"I need to talk to you about Rawr, but first I have something I need to take care of."

"What?"

"Scarlett was real antsy around that fallen tree trunk," Lacey said. "I want to go take a look at what she was reacting so strongly to."

Creed nodded. "I'll go out there with you."

She studied him for a moment, then gave a short dip of her head. "Can you keep Regina and the others here until we finish checking out that tree trunk?" she asked.

He narrowed his eyes. "Why? Don't tell me Scarlett is trained in cadaver search, as well."

Lacey shook her head. "She started out that way but hated it. She apparently just really did not like the smell and would be very skittish when she got close to a dead body."

"Can't say I blame her," he muttered.

"And she would sneeze. She was acting that way out by the tree."

Creed froze. "I see. And you think there's a dead body out there?"

"I don't *think* so. I'm...*afraid* so."

Lynette Eason is a bestselling, award-winning author who makes her home in South Carolina with her husband and two teenage children. She enjoys traveling, spending time with her family and teaching at various writing conferences around the country. She is a member of Romance Writers of America and American Christian Fiction Writers. Lynette can often be found online interacting with her readers. You can find her at Facebook.com/lynette.eason and on Twitter, @lynetteeason.

Books by Lynette Eason

Love Inspired Suspense

True Blue K-9 Unit

Wrangler's Corner

Visit the Author Profile page at LoveInspired.com for more titles.

FOLLOWING THE TRAIL

LYNETTE EASON

LOVE INSPIRED SUSPENSE

INSPIRATIONAL ROMANCE

LOVE INSPIRED® SUSPENSE
INSPIRATIONAL ROMANCE

ISBN-13: 978-1-335-73600-0

Following the Trail

Love Inspired
22 Adelaide St. West, 41st Floor
Toronto, Ontario M5H 4E3, Canada
www.LoveInspired.com

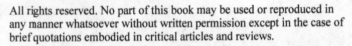

Printed in U.S.A.

For I know the thoughts that I think toward you,
saith the Lord, thoughts of peace, and not of evil,
to give you an expected end. Then shall ye call upon me,
and ye shall go and pray unto me, and I will hearken
unto you. And ye shall seek me, and find me,
when ye shall search for me with all your heart.
—*Jeremiah* 29:11-13

Dedicated to Jack Eason,
my husband and my everyday hero. I love you so much.

ONE

Lacey Lee Jefferson was worried. In fact, she was borderline terrified. Her sister, Fawn, had been silent for the past five days, not answering texts, emails or phone calls.

And Lacey'd had enough. She'd been avoiding calling Fawn's work because of her sister's strong stance about not receiving personal calls while on duty, but desperate times called for desperate measures. So, she'd called and learned Fawn, a doctor at the hospital, had taken a three-month absence, only to return to work for two days before dropping off the radar once more.

This morning, Lacey had made the three-hour journey out to her childhood home, where Fawn still lived, and had found it empty, with no indication where her sister might be.

Which was why Lacey now stood outside the sheriff's department in Timber Creek, North Carolina. Only her missing sister could have enticed her back to this town for the first time in six years. She pushed through the glass doors and made her way to the receptionist's desk, bracing herself for any animosity that might flare when the woman realized who stood in front of her. "Hi, Sherry."

Sherry Olson looked up from her computer screen and her eyes widened. "Well, as I live and breathe, if it isn't Lacey Lee."

"Just Lacey these days, thanks." Sherry and Lacey had graduated high school together. And as far as she could tell, there was nothing but surprise in Sherry's eyes. Relief nearly sent Lacey puddling to the floor.

"It's good to see you," Sherry said. "It's been a long time." Not long enough, as far as Lacey was concerned, but… "What can I do for you?"

"Have you seen Fawn lately?"

Sherry frowned. "No, not that I can think of, but we don't exactly run in the same circles. She's still working at the hospital, right?"

"Right. She was at work last week for two days, then never came back for her next shift. Before that, she'd taken a three-month leave of absence, but it's been a week now since anyone's heard from her."

"What? That doesn't sound like Fawn."

"No kidding. That's why I'm here. I want to talk to someone about doing a missing person report. Fawn's not answering her phone at all—or returning calls or texts. Everything goes straight to voice mail and I'm really getting worried." Understatement of the century.

"Oh my. That doesn't sound good." Sherry picked up the phone. "Creed, someone's out here to see you."

Creed? Creed Payne? Well, of course it would be Creed. He was the sheriff, after all. The sheriff with the smoky gray eyes and wavy dark hair, broad shoulders she'd cried on more than once as a teen. Creed... It disturbed her that her heart still sighed at his name.

Sherry hung up. "He said to send you on back to his office. Go down the hall and it's the last door on the left."

"Thanks."

Lacey knew exactly where Creed's office was. He'd brought her to this building when she was seventeen years old, shown her the corner office that the sheriff used and said, "That's going to be mine one day."

She'd thought it terribly shortsighted of him and told him he was meant for bigger things, that he was selling himself short.

"Thanks a lot, Lacey. Glad you think so much of my dreams." He'd shoved his hands into his pockets and stalked away.

Lacey had been crushed. Desperate to talk to him before she left for college, she'd gone home, packed up her car and called him again. His mother had answered the phone and said she didn't know where he was. Lacey had tried to find him, searched the whole town, but hadn't been able to locate him before she'd had to leave. And now she was going to talk to him for the first time in six years.

She raised her fist to knock when the door opened, and there he stood, larger-than-life. He was just as she remembered—and so much more. He'd filled out and become a man.

Their eyes met.

His widened.

Her heart thundered.

His lips parted, formed her name—

"Creed! Creed!"

He jerked his head at Sherry's shriek. "What is it?"

Sherry stood just in the hallway, her face pale, fist clutched around the phone. "Little Hank's missing. This is Joe, saying he and Denise can't find him. They've been searching for over half an hour."

Denise Banks and Joe Gilstrap from high school? They'd married? Fawn hadn't mentioned that.

"Where'd they last see him?" Creed

asked. Sherry held the phone out to him and he snatched it. "Joe? When did you last see Hank?... Uh-huh... Okay... I'm heading that way. Keep looking and I'll be there soon." He hung up and gave the phone back to Sherry. "Tell Ben."

She hurried back down the hall. Creed sighed and grabbed his Stetson from his desk. "Hank's five years old. Poor kid has wandered off and is probably scared to death. We need to find him before it gets dark."

"Want some help?" Lacey asked.

He narrowed his eyes. "Sure. We can use all the volunteers we can get."

"What about a search-and-rescue dog?"

"That's on the wish list. Unfortunately, we haven't raised the funds for it yet."

"No, I mean I have one. Scarlett's in the car."

He blinked at her for a good three seconds before he huffed a short laugh. "I really hope you're not kidding."

"Not kidding at all. She's a redbone coonhound with one of the best tracking noses in the country. I'm a contract K-9 handler for the Mecklenburg police department in Charlotte. When I'm not doing Search and Rescue operations, I have my own training facility with several volunteers and one part-time paid employee."

His jaw dropped. "How long have you been doing that?"

"For about three years."

"That's...incredible. Like an answer to prayer." He nodded. "Okay, then, let's get Scarlett and go find Hank."

"I'll just need something of Hank's to let her get the scent."

"I'll arrange it on the way."

"I'll follow you."

He strode out of the office and down the hall, his long legs eating up the distance. "Ben! Mac!"

"Coming!" Ben Land stepped out of his office. He spotted Lacey and his eyes widened. "Hey there, Lacey Lee. How are you?"

"It's just Lacey now, Ben. I'm doing fine." Mostly.

"Let's catch up after we find this kid."

"I'd love to." He'd always been kind to her in high school. More so than most after her father went to prison.

He looked at Creed. "Mac's not here, but he'll meet us there."

"Great."

Lacey hurried to her truck and waited for Creed and Ben to pull out of the parking lot. She fell in behind them, and Scarlett let out a yip from her spot in the back.

"You ready to go to work, girl?"

Two more barks answered her, and Lacey smiled before focusing her concentration on following the men up the mountain. About halfway to the top, Creed pulled into a long driveway that ended at a two-story log cabin home. The wooded area behind the house appeared to go on for infinity, but Lacey knew exactly what was on the other side of those woods.

Her sister's house.

Technically, it was half hers, too, but she'd not laid any claim to it. However,

Fawn loved their childhood home and had been happy to stay there while working at the hospital fifteen minutes away. Lacey hated it. All it did for her was symbolize loss and remind her of days she'd rather forget.

Goose bumps pebbled her skin, but she did her best to ignore them while she opened the door to Scarlett's customized back seat and snapped the lead to her collar.

The dog hopped down, her droopy ears flopping around her head while her tongue hung from the side of her mouth. Her dark eyes watched Lacey with expectation. "Hang on, girl."

More cars pulled up, and soon the front yard was full of townspeople ready to help search for little Hank.

"Lacey? Is that you?"

She turned to see Isabelle McGee headed toward her, followed by Katherine Gilroy—no, O'Ryan now, according to Fawn—one of the doctors in town. Lacey tensed, then allowed herself to relax slightly when she saw no condemnation in either pair of eyes. Interesting. She'd thought after what her father had done, the grudge would have been held infinitely. Had she been wrong? "Hey, how are you guys?"

"Good," Isabelle said. "What brings you back to town?"

"I'm looking for Fawn. Have either of you seen her lately?"

Isabelle shook her head and Katherine frowned. "I saw her last week at the hospital. I had to go in to see a patient and we passed in the hall. We didn't get a chance to chat, but I wanted to ask her if she was all right."

"Why?"

"She looked rough. Like she'd had too many sleepless nights or was getting over an illness. But we've been so busy that I haven't had a chance to catch up with her." And while Katherine and Fawn were both doctors and often in the hospital at the same time, they weren't close friends, so it wasn't likely Katherine would have thought any more about it.

"Okay, thanks."

"Isabelle?" A man about her age, dressed in the local deputy uniform, hurried toward them.

"That's Mac," Katherine said, her voice low.

"Isabelle's husband."

"Yes."

"Lacey, are you and Scarlett ready?" Creed hollered at her from the tree line.

"Ready!" She shot the two ladies a tight smile. "Do you mind asking some of the people here if they've seen or heard from Fawn? I'm getting desperately worried about her."

"Of course," Isabelle said. "I think I even still have your number in my phone, if it hasn't changed."

"It hasn't." She'd kept the same number for many reasons. One of those reasons stood waiting for her.

"I'll get it from Isabelle," Katherine said.

"Go find Hank, please. I'll be looking, too, in case he needs medical attention."

With a wave, Lacey darted toward Creed and the terrified parents. When she reached them, they all eyed Scarlett with flares of hope. "Thank you for doing this, Lacey." Denise's dark brows furrowed further. She had a small sleeping baby strapped to her chest. "When Creed called and said you were here with a search-and-rescue dog… Well, you're an answer to our prayers." She clasped her hands under the baby's rump. "You can really do this?"

"Scarlett and I can. I need something of Hank's that has his scent on it."

"Um, yeah," Joe said. "Creed told us what to get. Here." He passed her a bag. "It's the pajama shirt he wore last night."

"Perfect. Where did you last see him?"

"On the screened-in porch." Denise swiped the tears on her cheeks even as more fell. She patted the baby's back. "I needed to change the little man here, but hadn't brought a diaper out with me." She ran a shaking hand over the infant's head. "I'm just getting used to this whole two-children thing, and sometimes I forget..."

"It's okay, honey," Joe said. "This isn't on you."

Denise drew in a shuddering breath. "Anyway, I ran to get one and some wipes. When I came back, there was a hole in the screen and Hank was gone." A sob shook her, and Joe slid an arm around her shoulders.

Lacey's heart ached for the couple. "Could someone have taken him?" If he'd been put in a car...

"No," Joe said. "We have security cameras, and the footage showed him kicking the screen out and walking away. He's a curious kid..."

Well, that was better than being snatched. "All right. So, what I'm going to do is give Scarlett a whiff of this, then kind of walk her around until she picks up the trail."

Denise nodded, and while Joe looked a little skeptical, his expression held a desperate hope.

The long lead attached to Scarlett's harness would allow the dog the freedom to run at a pretty good pace while Lacey followed. Lacey tapped her pocket and Scarlett fairly danced with excitement. She knew as soon as she did her job, she'd get to play with her favorite toy. A tennis ball.

Lacey opened the bag with Hank's shirt and held it for the animal. "Scarlett, seek."

Scarlett stuck her snout in the opening and got her whiff.

"Scarlett, seek. Find Hank."

Scarlett's tail wagged, and she lifted her head, black nose quivering, ears waving in the wind. With a short bark, she started pacing, alternating nose in the air and near the ground. Soon, she gave another bark and took off like a shot for the woods.

"Here we go," Lacey said. She followed Scarlett at a fast jog, her hand wrapped around the end of the lead. Footsteps fell into place behind her. She shot a quick glance back and noted Creed's expression.

He was coming along whether she wanted him to or not.

Too bad he hadn't felt that way six years ago.

Creed couldn't help that his heart beat faster. Not just because he was jogging after Lacey and Scarlett, and not just because a child was in danger. But because Lacey Lee—Lacey now, he reminded himself—was back in town.

Lacey. He'd thought he'd moved on from the heartbreak she'd caused him, but all it had taken to bring it back was to find her standing outside his office door.

Sherry's timely interruption had kept him from blurting out something he might've later regretted. He honestly had no idea what he'd been about to say, and now he'd probably never know. He was okay with that. But when she hadn't hesitated to offer her help to find Hank, he'd found himself admiring her all over again.

No. He had no intention of getting involved with Lacey this time. Not that she'd offered him the opportunity. He didn't even know how long she'd been in town before she'd stopped in to the station. And he had no idea why she was there. He ordered his heart to chill, forbade it from yearning for something that was so far in the past he shouldn't even remember the slightest detail.

But he did.

He watched her lithe form dodge trees and undergrowth while she kept a steady pace. She'd done this many times before and seemed to excel at it. That could only work in Hank's favor. *Please, God, protect that little boy. Please let us find him alive and just fine.*

They had to. He refused to think of the alternative. Lacey pulled to a stop while Scarlett walked in circles. "What is it?" he asked.

"She's not sure which way to go."

"We're almost to your property line."

"I know."

The dog walked to a fallen tree trunk, sniffed and shook herself. Barked and backed up, whining, then sneezed twice. Lacey's frown took on a deeper, more intense look. Then Scarlett walked back to Lacey and looked up at her, sad eyes pleading for help. She really wanted to find the person attached to the scent. Lacey opened the bag with the pajama top and let Scarlett get another sniff.

"She okay?"

"Yes. I think so." Her gaze lingered on the tree trunk, a stormy look in her eyes.

"Lacey?"

She blinked and nodded. "Yes. She still has his scent." As though she understood, the dog spun off in the direction toward Lacey's old home. "This way," Lacey said.

"I'm right behind you."

He stayed with her and Scarlett, with the dog weaving back and forth, nose in the air. Then she stopped. Barked once and made a beeline for the old shed at the back of Lacey's property.

"Think he went in there?" Creed asked, starting to feel slightly winded at the fast pace. Lacey looked like she could go another few miles.

"I don't know. Dad always kept it locked, but Fawn may not have." They reached the shed while Scarlett nosed the walls. "She definitely wants to go in."

Creed followed Lacey around to the door. "Weird. The lock is still on there," she said. "I don't know why she'd want in if Hank's not in there."

He passed her, his gaze scanning the structure. "Hank? Can you hear me? If you can, answer. I want to take you home to your mama and daddy. They're waiting on you."

Silence.

"Hank?" Lacey called. Scarlett continued her attempts to find an entrance to the building.

Creed stopped. A little blue blanket lay on the ground next to one of the boards. He pressed on the plank and the bottom of it swung inward. "Lacey? Over here." She hurried to him.

He nodded to the blanket. "It's possible

Hank crawled through and couldn't get back out."

Scarlett ducked down and scrambled through the hole.

"Hold the board, will you?" Lacey asked.

He did and she crawled after Scarlett. Creed knelt and peered inside. There was no way he'd fit. "Lacey? You see him?"

"Yeah! He's here. Pull the board off. I'm going to pass him through to you."

"Is he okay?" Creed jerked the board off and the two beside it. When he looked inside, he could see Lacey with the child in her arms. Hank's head rested on her shoulder.

"Hey, little man," she said, her voice low and soft. Comforting. "You sure have a lot of people looking for you."

"I want my mama," the boy said. A tear tracked down his filthy cheek and Lacey brushed it away. Hank lifted his head and rubbed his eyes. "I got lost-ed."

"I know, sweetie. We're going to take you to see your mama right now, okay?"

"'Kay. I like the doggy. He *lick-ted* me."

"*He's* a *she*," Lacey said. "Her name's Scarlett, and she's been looking for you."

Hank yawned, and Scarlett stood on her hind legs to nudge him, pulling a giggle from the little guy.

Lacey looked up and her eye caught Creed's. "He's cold and a little pale, but he found a spot at the back of the shed and crawled under a tarp. He's got a few scrapes, but nothing major. I'm sure he's hungry, but overall, I'd say he's none the worse for wear for this adventure."

Creed unzipped his jacket and shrugged out of it. The wind bit at him, but he'd survive. Lacey picked her way through the old tools and passed him the little boy. Creed set him on his feet for a brief moment while he wrapped the big coat around him like a blanket, then lifted him into his arms. *Thank You, Jesus.* The prayer whispered from his lips and his heart lightened exponentially. "I'm sure glad to see you, kid."

"Hi, Mr. Sheriff. Can I go home now?" Creed knew Hank from church, and the little guy had dubbed him Mr. Sheriff from the moment they'd met. He had no idea why, but he was fine with the title.

"Yeah, that sounds like a really good idea."

Hank snuggled down against him. "I'm tired and hungry. I want some pizza and apple juice and a big bag of naminal cookies."

At Lacey's raised brow, Creed translated. "Animal cookies."

"Oh, right. Of course." She patted Hank's back. "I'm pretty sure your mom and dad are going to give you just about whatever you want right now."

Hank didn't answer and Creed smiled. "He's asleep."

"Wow. That was fast."

"Kids."

She shuddered. "There are a lot of things in that shed that he could have hurt himself on. I'm so glad he's okay."

"Me, too. Why don't we let his parents know?" Creed pulled his phone out of his pocket and used one hand to dial Joe's number. "We found him," he said in lieu of a greeting. "And he's just fine. Sleeping on my shoulder. Jump in your car and meet us at Lacey and Fawn's place. We'll be waiting on you inside."

Lacey started to lead the way when a sharp crack echoed around them and the dirty window of the shed exploded.

TWO

Lacey let out a short cry and dropped to the ground. Creed hit his knees as well while he hunched over the child in his arms. "Get behind the building!" The second shot hit the wooden side of the structure. "Go!"

He grabbed her arm, and Lacey shoved to her feet and bolted around the corner of the shed. Scarlett followed. "Scarlett, down." The dog dropped and watched Lacey with intent eyes. "Stay." Creed huddled next to her while trying to dial one-handed. "Give me Hank," she said.

Without waiting for him to answer, she pulled the boy into her arms, and he looked up with a frown. "Am I home?"

"No, baby. Go back to sleep." Hank gave a disgruntled sigh but dropped his head to her shoulder. She eyed Creed, who had his weapon in his hand and was peering around the corner with the phone pressed to his ear. "Was someone shooting at us?" She hiss-whispered the words.

"Definitely. Thankfully, they appear to be a bad shot."

"But...why?" She could hear the phone ringing.

"I have no id— Ben, we've got a shooter out at the Jefferson place. You and Mac get out here with some backup, will you?... Yeah... Tell Joe and Denise to hang back until we make sure the shooter's gone, but reassure them that Hank's fine. And we plan on keeping him that way."

He hung up and silence greeted them. No more gunshots. No movement that she could discern. "Could have been a hunter, maybe?"

"This is private property," Creed said. "Not that some people care about that..."

Sirens sounded. She tucked little Hank closer and checked on Scarlett. She was still and quiet as she'd been ordered to do, although when Scarlett caught her watching, she crawled forward and nudged Lacey as though asking if everything was all right. Lacey scratched the dog's ears. "Stay."

Because they were huddled behind the building at the back of the house, she couldn't see the cruiser pull in, but the blue lights flashed their arrival.

Footsteps pounded toward them and Hank roused once more. "I wanna see my mama. You said you were taking me to my mama. Where is she?"

"She's here, Hank. Just hold on a few more minutes. Please?"

"Why?"

"Because we have to make sure it's safe."

His eyes widened slightly and a shiver ran through him, but she wasn't going to lie to him. He was old enough to understand what it meant for an adult to want to make sure the situation was safe for him.

"Mama! I want my mama now!" His top-of-his-lungs scream pierced her eardrums. So, he might be old enough to understand, but that didn't mean he had to like it, of course. He struggled to get out of her hold and she had to squeeze him tighter than she would have liked.

He screeched again and Creed spun to take him from her. "Hank, stop it."

Hank froze midscream. Creed didn't raise his voice, but the firm tone reached through to the little boy. Then tears filled his eyes and spilled over his dirty cheeks. Lacey's heart nearly broke for the child. All he wanted was his mother.

"Creed!" Ben's shout reached them.

"Be careful, Ben. I don't know where the shooter is."

"Regina and Mac are out there looking but need some direction. Where'd the bullets come from?"

"One took out the window on the other side of the building. The second hit the wall. So I'd say east." He glanced around the corner and Lacey figured he was trying to discern exactly where to send the other deputies. "There's a pocket of trees just past the little horse pasture. It's in direct line with the building."

"Stay there until I give you the all clear."

"Copy that." Creed looked at Lacey. "You okay?"

"Yeah." She nodded to Hank. "Looks like he is, too."

He'd fallen back to sleep on Creed's shoulder.

"Creed?" Ben's voice came over the radio. "Yeah?"

"We're here at the clearing," Regina said. "There are signs that someone was definitely here. The underbrush is stirred up pretty good, and there's an indentation in the ground like someone knelt here. But there are no discernible footprints or anything like that. On the first pass, there's no real evidence to collect. Whoever pulled the trigger picked up any casings."

"All right," Creed said, "nothing we can do about it now." He paused. "Hang out up there for the next few minutes. Just until we get this little one delivered back to his family."

"Sure thing."

Creed caught Lacey's eye. "Let's get Hank into his mama's arms."

"Works for me." Lacey stepped around the building, called for Scarlett to heel and headed for the house.

Creed fell into step beside her. "That was some pretty impressive work you and Scarlett did out there."

"Thanks. It's what we've trained for."

"I know. I guess I'm trying to figure out how to ask you something."

"What's that?"

"Do you want a job?"

Creed shut his mouth so fast, he nearly bit his tongue. Had he really just offered employment to the woman who'd broken his heart? There was no way he wanted to be stuck working with her day in and day out, a constant reminder of how she'd chosen the big city over him—over them. Then again, she could accuse him of doing the same thing to her.

But that was different. This was his home.

And hers, too, whether she wanted to admit it or not.

She laughed, her green eyes crinkling at the corners. "Um…no, but thanks."

"Seriously," he found himself saying, "it would be full-time with benefits and everything."

"As what, Creed?"

"A deputy. And leader of the K-9 unit."

"You don't have a K-9 unit."

"We would if you started one."

She gaped at him.

"Hank!" The frantic cry stopped any reply she might have been forming.

"Mama!" The little boy jerked up and around, nearly tumbling out of Creed's grasp. Only his quick reflexes kept him from dropping the kid. Instead, he lowered him to the ground and the child shrugged the heavy coat off and closed the gap to throw himself into his mother's arms. Joe was right there holding his wife and child close, tears streaming down his cheeks.

Creed's heart clenched as he was reminded once more why he stayed in this small town. Because he was good at his job and these people needed him to be here.

Regina, Ben and Mac joined them, their matching frowns telling him more about what they'd found—or rather, hadn't found—up on the mountain.

They approached while Lacey pulled out a tennis ball and gave it a toss toward an empty space in her massive yard. Scarlett took off like a shot, her sheer joy in the reward bringing a smile to his face. He looked back at Regina and Ben, his lips turning down. "Nothing?"

"No." Regina shook her head. "Sorry."

Ben shrugged. "Maybe it was a hunter who ran when he realized what he'd done."

"Or she," Regina said.

Ben dipped his head. "Right. Or she. And I'll just say that the location the person picked was pretty much perfect. He—or she—had a good line of sight for the shed. And a lot of the area around it, including the house and the driveway."

"So," Creed said, "probably a hunter

waiting for a buck to put in an appearance." What else could it be? "All right, let's get back to the station and get the paperwork all done."

He turned to Lacey. "I guess we need to chat."

Lacey raised a brow at him. "Chat?"

"You were coming to see me for a reason. And the reason got interrupted by our hunt for Hank."

Her expression darkened. "Yes, I need to talk to you about Fawn, but first, I have something I need to take care of."

"What?"

"Scarlett was real antsy around that fallen tree trunk," she said. "I want to go take a look at what she was reacting so strongly to."

Creed nodded. "I'll go out there with you, and we can talk on the way."

Lacey studied him for a moment, then gave a short dip of her head. "Can you keep Regina and the others here until we finish checking out that tree trunk?" she asked.

He narrowed his eyes. "Why? Don't tell me Scarlett is trained in cadaver search, as well."

Lacey shook her head. "She started out that way but hated it and was terrible at it. She apparently just really did not like the smell and would be very skittish when she got close to a dead body."

"Can't say I blame her," he muttered.

"And she would sneeze. She was acting that way out by the tree."

Creed froze. "I see. And you think there's a dead body out there?"

"I don't *think* so. I'm…*afraid* so."

THREE

And she was afraid to think who it might be. But the feeling in her gut told her to prepare herself. Lacey snapped the leash onto Scarlett's harness and started off toward the woods. She didn't have anything for Scarlett to sniff, so she simply acted like they were going for a walk. Scarlett was completely fine with that.

"Tell me about Fawn," Creed said, shortening his long stride to match hers. "What's going on with her?"

"She's missing, as far as I can tell. We text just about every day, even if it's just a short 'Hey, hope you have a good day' kind of text. We miss a day here and there, especially since Fawn's work at the hospital has her on some erratic hours and she has to sleep during some of my awake hours, but when the third day went by with no word from her, I got concerned. It's been five days, and I've gone past concerned straight into scared to death for her." Especially considering how Scarlett had been acting around that one particular area this close to home.

"What about your mom? Has she heard anything?"

"No—and she was one of the first people I asked, but she and Fawn don't really talk. Fawn didn't agree with this new marriage and was giving Mom the silent treatment. I think the last time they communicated was on Fawn's birthday six months ago. I'm not keeping Mom in the loop on this. Not until I know something definite."

"Ouch."

"Yes, but Mom marches to her own drummer." She glanced at him. "Fawn's a lot like our mother in that sense. The things that bother her don't bother me. And vice versa."

Before he could respond, Scarlett stopped

and bayed. Then raced back to Lacey, shaking her head and sneezing, tugging on the leash to get away from the area. "That's her 'alert' that there's a dead body, and I just don't know if I can…look."

"You're afraid it's Fawn."

"Yes." *Please don't be, please don't be. Please, God, don't let it be my sister.*

He nodded. "Stand back and let me see what I can see."

Lacey hesitated, then held back, leading Scarlett away from the area. She was more than happy to follow Lacey, who tied her lead to a limb, then walked back over to join Creed, who was scouting the tree. He looked up. "Okay, looks like this trunk is covering something up. I'm trying to figure out a way to move the trunk without disturbing anything that might be underneath. Why don't you go stay with Scarlett?"

She curled her fingers into fists. "I can help."

He eyed her. "You sure?"

"We're trained in this kind of thing. Let's

do it right. If my sister is the one—" She pulled in a steadying breath. "Or even if it's not her and it's someone else, they deserve respect and justice."

"And there's no way it could be an animal?"

Lacey raised a brow. "You know better than that."

"Yeah, I do, but you can't blame a guy for hoping."

"Dogs know the difference. They can track the scent of a decomposing human while ignoring the dead squirrel in their path. It's truly amazing." She met his eyes. He knew all that, but talking was helping keep her heartbeat from flying out of her chest. "No, there's a dead person down there. The freezing temps are just keeping us from smelling it."

He nodded. "I believe you."

She motioned to the wood. "I'll get this end if you'll grab that one."

He gripped the trunk with his gloved hands. Lacey did the same on her side, and together they shifted the heavy wood away and set it to the side.

When she looked down into the shallow grave, her breath caught. The body was face down, rolled to her side, but she had long auburn hair and was dressed in a lab coat. The blue-and-white bracelet encircling her right wrist sealed it for Lacey.

She pressed her lips together and met Creed's eyes. "It's her." *Hold it together. Don't cry. Don't—* Tears leaked, splashing over her lashes and onto her cheeks. "Aw, Creed, it's Fawn. I g-gave her that bracelet for her b-birthday."

His arms came around her just as her knees gave out. He lowered her to the ground and pulled her close, burying her face against his chest. "I'm sorry, Lacey. I'm so sorry."

A sob ripped from her. She fisted the material of his coat and bit off the other cries that wanted to escape. She pulled herself together, even while wondering if her heart would ever feel whole again.

* * *

Creed let his heart break with hers. He'd known Fawn all her life, and while they hadn't been close in the past few years, he'd considered her a friend.

Lacey pulled back, scrubbing the tears from her eyes. "I'm sorry."

"Lacey, please." He cupped her chin. "You don't have anything to be sorry for. I... I don't even know what to say. This is beyond awful..." He let her go, and Scarlett whined from her spot, tugging at her lead.

Lacey walked over to the dog, dropped to her knees and buried her face in the sleek brown coat. When she drew in a shuddering breath and pulled back, Scarlett swiped her tongue over Lacey's cheek. Creed waited, giving her another moment, then said, "I'm going to have to call the medical examiner and a crime scene unit."

"I know." She stood and met his gaze. The agony there nearly killed him.

He took her hand. "Cry if you need to."

"I'll cry later," she said, her voice hoarse. "For now, we need to take care of Fawn."

He gave a slow nod. "All right. Come on."

She and Scarlett followed him back to the edge of the woods. He'd have to guide the others to the body. Fawn. She wasn't just a body. She'd been a person, a sister, a daughter, a friend, a respected member of the medical community, and more. His throat tightened and he cleared it. "I know it's painful, Lacey, but did Fawn have any enemies you can think of?"

"No, not offhand." She paused and swiped a stray tear. "I don't know how she died, Creed, but her death wasn't an accident. She didn't crawl in that little wooded area and pull that trunk over the hiding place. This has all the signs that someone killed her and didn't want her found."

"I agree."

"I thought you did when you asked if she had any enemies. Sorry. I don't know why I felt compelled to point it out."

He squeezed her shoulder. "It's fine, Lacey."

While they waited for the crime scene unit, Regina, Ben and Mac hurried over to meet them. Creed gave them the rundown of what they'd found and the deputies paled.

"Wait a minute," Ben said. "I saw Fawn at the hospital a couple of days ago. She looked worn-out and I commented that she needed a vacation. She said she'd just had one and was glad to be back at work."

"What day was that?" Creed asked.

"Um… Tuesday, I think."

"That's the last day I heard from her," Lacey said, her features pinched. "She never let on that anything was wrong—if anything *was* at that point."

Creed guided Lacey out of the way of the gurney. The medical examiner nodded, his eyes shadowed. "Lacey. Heard you were back."

"Hi, Zeb. Yeah, I'm back. For now," she said. "Word travels fast in Timber Creek.

I guess some things never change." Lacey knew everyone in town, just like Creed.

Because most people who grew up in Timber Creek only left for a short time before finding their way back. Or they never left at all.

Except Lacey. She'd left and would be leaving again.

He shook the thoughts from his head. Dwelling on the past and dreading the future weren't going to accomplish anything helpful in the present. While they waited, Zeb examined the area of the body he could see, collected anything that he thought might be evidence and then directed Regina and Ben on how to extract the body.

Once Fawn was in the body bag and on the gurney, Zeb directed Ben and Mac to help put her in the back of the coroner's van, then walked over to join Creed and Lacey.

"I'm really sorry, Lacey."

She nodded and absently scratched Scarlett's ears. The thump, thump, thump of helicopter blades caught her attention, and she looked up to see a news chopper hovering overhead. Far enough not to disturb the area, but their cameras were good. "Creed?"

"I see them." He pulled his phone from his pocket and barked orders about getting rid of the bird while Lacey's gaze stayed on the van until the doors were shut.

Creed stomped back over, his face twisted in a scowl. The helicopter banked off and he shook his head. "Vultures."

The chopper forgotten, Lacey turned her eyes to Zeb. "How did she die?"

Zeb hesitated, then met Creed's eyes. Creed gave a fraction of a nod and Zeb sighed. "It looks like she was hit in the head with a blunt object."

At Lacey's sharp gasp, Creed squeezed her fingers. "Thanks, Zeb," she said, her voice so low he barely heard it. "Take care of her."

"The best." He looked at Creed. "I'll be in touch." He paused. "I'll let you know now that I'm the only ME at the moment and I'm backed up on cases. The other doc took a job in Arizona and left without notice. It may take me a while to get to her. I'm not talking weeks, but possibly a couple of days. I'll do a preliminary scan and see if I can locate anything that can be run through the systems, like DNA or hair or fibers or whatever, but the actual autopsy will have to wait a while."

Creed nodded. "Understood."

He left and Lacey didn't move until the van was out of sight. Then she clicked to Scarlett and started walking.

"Where are you going?" Creed asked.

"To get my SUV and bring it back to the house."

"Okay. Anything I can do to help?" He wasn't ready to let her out of his sight yet. She'd just had a major tragedy, and he wasn't sure she was thinking clearly.

"Help? I don't know, Creed." She drew in a shuddering breath. "All I know right now is that I came home to find her, and I have. Now I need to find her killer, and I'm not leaving here until I do."

"That's my job, Lacey. My department's job."

"That offer of a job still stand?"

He had a feeling he knew where this was going. "Yes."

"Then let's try things this way. I'll take a leave of absence from my current position and work with you on a contract basis until we find Fawn's killer—and see what we can do about starting a K-9 unit." She paused. "As long as my boss is willing, I'll stay until you have at least one handler on board. After that, well, we'll just have to see where we are at that point. If you're agreeable."

"I'm agreeable. Welcome to the Timber Creek Sheriff's Office."

FOUR

"But?" she asked.

"But you know as well as I do—you can't investigate your sister's death," he said, his voice soft, falling into step beside her.

"Not officially, anyway. I know." She stopped walking and he turned to face her. "But if I'm part of the department," she said, "I can be privy to information you wouldn't tell me otherwise."

He studied her for a moment, his eyes shadowed, unreadable, but he finally nodded. "All right. We'll get the paperwork all drawn up and finalized. I really do want to start a K-9 program. That can be your job while you're here. Not investigating Fawn's murder."

"I get it, I promise." She started walking again. Her head pounded with the thought of everything she was going to have to deal with in the coming weeks. "I need to call my boss and let him know what's going on and ask for some time off."

"Of course."

Lacey made the call, his heart breaking all over again as he listened to her explain the situation. When she hung up, she bit her lip. "What could she have done for someone to do this to her?"

He shook his head. "If you don't know, I sure don't. You said you were texting with her right up until a few days ago."

"Right."

"And she never let on that there was anything wrong?"

"No." She paused. "Not verbally, anyway."

"What does that mean?"

"It means that she never said anything was wrong, but I sensed something. I asked her about it a couple of times. She said everything was fine. I thought she sounded weird, but then it would pass. I figured she'd fill me in when she was ready. If there was anything to fill me in on. I really just thought she was tired from work." Tears threatened and she only managed to keep them at bay through sheer willpower. "*Now* I keep asking myself if what I thought I was sensing has to do with her death." She shook her head. "Why didn't I press her for answers?"

"You think she would have told you if you had?"

"I don't know. And, honestly, at the time, a part of me was relieved that she didn't give me another problem to deal with." She bit her lip and looked away. She'd never forgive herself for not getting in the car and making the trip to confront Fawn about whatever it was she was hiding.

"Come on, Lace—"

"No, I'm serious. I've been under so much stress at work and I just couldn't... deal with anything else. I told myself that once I was out from all the pressure at work, I'd figure out what was going on with Fawn. So, that's on me."

"You worked a lot?"

"All the time. Literally. I ate on the run and slept when I could. The demand for well-trained dogs is high and I was training left and right. I was also working shifts with Scarlett with the department and it seemed like I was getting at least one call every day." Lacey raked a hand over her ponytail and pulled it tighter. "But Fawn knew she could tell me anything. And if she needed me, all she had to do was say the word, and stress or no stress, work or no work, I would have dropped everything to be here for her. She *knew* that." Lacey paused. "At least, I thought she did."

They'd reached her SUV, and Scarlett raced to her door to sit and wait.

"She's an amazing animal," Creed said.

"Thanks. We've spent many hours working and training." And just maybe that training would be something she could use to her advantage when it came to finding Fawn's killer.

"You did a great job with her."

"I appreciate that." Lacey opened the door and Scarlett hopped up to settle in her spot. The dog sighed and placed her nose between her paws while her dark brown eyes bounced between Lacey and Creed.

"I'm impressed," Creed said, "although I guess I shouldn't be. You've always loved dogs and planned to go into law enforcement." His gaze touched lightly over her features. "You're probably way overqualified for this little town. I'm not sure it can afford you."

"Well, right now, you don't have to worry about it. I'm here until we find Fawn's killer and set up your K-9 unit."

"Good. I'll follow you home—er... I mean, to Fawn's house." He sighed and paused. "I assume you're staying there?"

She pressed her fingers to her eyes. "I hadn't thought that far ahead, but yes, I guess I am. Doesn't make sense that I would pay for a hotel when the house is now mine." Just saying the words out loud made her nauseous.

"See you there."

Five minutes later, she walked back into her childhood home, and Creed was right behind her. She stopped just inside the foyer and took in the details. The dining room was to her left and had been redone to the point that she didn't recognize it. And yet she did. In front of her, the wall that had separated the den and kitchen had been removed to create one big open space.

Just a few hours earlier, she'd stopped in only long enough to verify that Fawn wasn't there before she'd dashed off to the sheriff's office. In those brief moments she'd been inside, she'd noted the differences Fawn had made in her efforts to restore the old farmhouse, but now Lacey paused and took in the details while she fought the grief clawing at her. "The windows still need the blinds put up. They're stacked over there next to the fireplace. I guess that was her next project."

"At least she has sheets over the windows for now."

"Yes." Lacey fell silent for a moment, then shook her head. "She always loved this old place."

"But you didn't."

"I did at first. But then came to hate it, as you well know."

"Lacey," he said, his husky voice a soothing balm to her battered spirit, "your father's actions shouldn't—"

She whirled. "I don't talk about him." At his flinch, she sucked in a breath. "Sorry, I didn't mean to snap, but please, don't bring him up again."

He frowned but nodded and cleared his throat. "Fawn was really making some good progress here, wasn't she?"

Lacey's shoulders relaxed a fraction. "She always said if medicine hadn't been her calling, she would have loved her own design show." Again, her throat tightened, and she fought to keep her feelings from showing. For years, she'd learned how to bury her emotions. She didn't need them getting in the way now. "Last week, when I talked to her, she said she was almost finished with the kitchen." Lacey walked through into the den and noted the kitchen area to her left. Granite countertops had replaced the peeling laminate. The wood floors had been redone, and stainless steel appliances now graced the spaces where the old yellow sixties ones had been. "She sure was enjoying that gas stove," Lacey said. "She hated the old electric range with the uneven burners."

"She was doing all this herself?"

"She and a few friends who were helping her out."

"What friends?"

"Danny Main was doing the electrical for her, and Nancy Stone was in charge of the plumbing."

He pointed to cans of paint next to the wall. "They're labeled. She picked different colors for each room?"

Lacey looked at the cans.

"She did. She told me each room was going to be a different color, even though there was only a very subtle difference in shade. I pointed out that she was going to have to change her rollers and clean everything in between." She gave a small laugh that she had to bite off before it turned into a sob. She cleared her throat. "But that was Fawn. She didn't care about minor inconveniences like that. She had more patience than I'll ever have."

Lacey walked down the hall toward the master bedroom. Creed and Scarlett followed, letting her set the pace. "Fawn did everything necessary to make the house livable before doing the blinds and paint. That was smart. As for help, I think Carol Malone was going to help her paint, but yeah, Fawn was doing the majority of it." She drew in a shaky breath. "I don't understand her need to stay here, but she was a lot like you. She wasn't leaving."

"People needed her here—or she thought they did."

"Yeah, I didn't get that either. After the way we were treated—after my father—" Ugh. She'd just snapped his head off for bringing the man up, and now she was doing it. "It was hard." She paused and let her gaze roam the room again. "The only reason this house wasn't taken to pay off my father's debts when he went to prison was because it was in my mom's name." She shot him a sad smile. "Did you know that?"

"Yeah. Mom mentioned it. Said she was glad that y'all still had a roof over your heads."

She fell silent while she led the way to the second floor. To the right had been her old room. She went to the door and pushed it open and flipped the light switch on. All of the furniture had been removed, except for a desk situated in the middle of the room, facing the window. "When he went to prison," she finally said, "I just..." She stopped and shuddered. "He betrayed everyone in this town, and people seemed to think the rest of us were just like him, waiting to steal whatever they had left."

He frowned. "Wait a minute, now. Come on, Lacey. You don't really believe that."

She laughed, then winced at the pain the

sound held. "Yes, I do. And you know it's true."

"I'm sorry," he said. "Deeply sorry."

"For what?"

"For...not noticing that. You obviously believe it's true about the town thinking ill of you, but I never... I just..."

"Didn't see it."

"Yeah."

"Because everyone loved you and your family. You had no reason to see it."

His frown deepened and he tilted his head. "I don't know if I agree with that, Lacey."

"It's okay. You don't have to." She shot him a small smile and gave a slight shrug. "I also think Fawn thought she owed it to the people in town to stay." Lacey covered a yawn, exhaustion mingling with her grief. "Sorry. I'm a bit wiped."

"Understandable." He started to say something, then stopped.

"What?" Lacey asked.

"Did Fawn say that? That she owed it to the townspeople to stay? Because that's—" he sighed "—wrong. Look, you said not to talk about your father, but—"

"I brought him up, so I guess I can't complain."

"Right. Look, he did a really rotten thing—"

"He stole from people who trusted him. That's a bit more than a rotten thing." Her father had been a well-respected financial adviser. Until he'd been caught fleecing his clients—most of whom had been friends. Some who had children the same ages as Lacey and Fawn.

"Well, you were right about one thing. Some things really don't ever change," he said, his tone wry.

She blinked. "What?" It hit her. She'd just interrupted him twice. "Oh. Sorry."

He shot her a smile. One tinged with sadness, regret and...longing? He blinked and the look was gone, leaving her to wonder if she'd imagined it. He walked to the window and pushed it open. With a glance back at her, he climbed out.

"What are you doing?" she asked.

"Sitting. Remembering the good times we had out here."

Remembering the conversations that lasted for hours? The talking about their futures? The sweet kisses that always ended too soon? She walked over and looked out. "You're right. Those weren't just good times. Those were the best." She laughed. "I interrupted you an awful lot out here." She climbed out to sit beside him.

"I never minded your interruptions, Lacey."

The tenderness in his voice nearly took her breath away. "Well, it's a lousy habit that I thought I'd broken, but five seconds back in Timber Creek and I'm right back where I started. Unbelievable."

"Like I said, I never minded. Still don't."

"Well, I do." She scrubbed her burning eyes with her palms. "Fawn used to get so mad at me for that." A sob caught in her throat, then escaped. "Oh, Creed, what am I going to do without her?"

His arms came around her as the next cry slipped out.

* * *

Like a lot of men, Creed had never been comfortable with a crying woman, but this was Lacey, and she'd cried on his shoulder more than once as a teen. He'd even cried on hers a time or two. Right in this very spot. So, now, while she let the grief flow, he let his long-held anger and hurt slide to the back burner.

He pulled her close and let her sob out her grief, wishing he had the words to help. But he didn't. Lacey finally sniffed and swiped a hand over her face before he could offer the hem of his shirt.

Scarlett walked to the window and poked her head out, her eyes never leaving her mistress's face. "She's okay, girl," Creed said, his voice soft. He scratched the dog behind her ears, and while she seemed to appreciate the reassurance, he wasn't sure she was convinced. Scarlett hopped out onto the roof and placed a paw on Lacey's knee.

Lacey choked on another sob and then lowered her forehead to the dog's. Finally, her heart-wrenching cries faded and she stilled. Then sniffed. Creed held his arm out. "Wanna use my sleeve?"

She choked on a half laugh, half sob and shook her head. Instead, she used her own shirt and he gave her some time to get herself together.

"I'm sorry, Lacey. I feel kind of helpless here. Tell me what to do."

She shook her head. "You did it. You let me cry without feeling self-conscious about it." She stood, slipped back into the room, trailed by Scarlett, and simply stood there. "Let's check the rest of the house. I don't think she did any structural changes up here. Not like downstairs."

He followed her to the other two bedrooms and bathrooms, then back down to the master. "There," she said. "I noticed that, but it didn't hit me how weird it was."

"What?"

"The dresser drawer. It's open." She walked over to it and pulled the drawer fully out. "And that's even more weird."

"Can you explain?"

"You know Fawn was a neat freak. She'd never leave a drawer cracked and she always kept her clothes just so. But these T-shirts are unfolded and…well, it looks like she just dumped them in here."

"Maybe she was in a hurry or something."

"No." She opened the drawer beneath it. "This is the same way."

"You think someone searched them?"

"Maybe. I don't know. Nothing else in the house looked off, so…" She shrugged.

His phone buzzed. "I hate to do this, but I've got to go. Regina, Ben and Mac are still out at the scene and I want to go have a look before it gets dark. Do you have anyone you can call to stay with you tonight?"

She looked up from the drawer. "I could call Jessica Hill, I guess."

"You still talk to her?"

"Not often, but we keep up. Exchange Christmas cards and such. I agreed to be in her wedding because it wasn't here." Jessica and Lacey had been best friends in high school. "She's one of the few people in this town who didn't make me feel like a pariah after Dad went to prison. But... she just had a baby not too long ago, so she might not be the best person either."

"What about Miranda Glenn?" Creed asked.

"Think she just had a baby, too, didn't she? She was closer to Fawn, anyway, but..." She dragged the word out. "She'd be a good one to talk to and see if Fawn said anything to her about any issues she may have been having—and hiding from me." Hurt flashed in those eyes he'd once thought he'd spend a lifetime staring into, and just like when they were teens, he wanted to be the one to take the pain away. To be her hero. But she'd rejected him back then, made it clear that he wasn't the priority in her life.

He cleared his throat. "I really need to go. I'll check on you after I finish at the scene."

"And let me know what you find?"

"If there's anything found, we'll talk."

"Thank you, Creed." She rubbed her eyes. "I guess I'll look around the house and see if there's anything that will give me a clue as to what was going on with her and where she was the last three months before I call Jessica. Even if I don't stay with her, it would be good to check in with her and see if she'd seen Fawn."

"Good idea. Let me know if you find anything."

"Of course." She nodded and he headed for the door. Once he was in his SUV, he sat there for a moment, reading text updates from Regina. He'd admit texting had its benefits, but he'd much rather talk on the phone. He dialed her number.

"Creed," she answered midring. "I assume you got my messages."

"I did. I'm on the way."

"See you when you get here."

It didn't take him long to reach the area. In fact, if Lacey looked out of her kitchen window, she'd be able to see the law enforcement vehicles still on her property. The crime scene unit had finally arrived, and he recognized Garrett Smith, the lead investigator. Garrett waved him over and Creed joined him at the spot Regina, Ben and Mac had found earlier.

He pulled little blue bootees on over his shoes and signed the log. Being careful where he stepped, Creed walked over to stand close to where the shooter had been and looked out, through the trees, straight at the shed in Lacey's backyard. And if he turned just enough, he could see the area where Fawn had been buried. "If you were going to kill someone," he said, "why bury her on her own property?"

Garrett shrugged. "I don't know. I wouldn't."

Creed looked at Regina. "Give me some scenarios that would make you do that. I have a few that I can come up with, but—" he shrugged "—humor me."

"The only thing I can think of is if the killer did the deed, then panicked. Buried the body and hoped no one would come looking this far from the house."

"But with a dog, she was easy to find."

Regina frowned. "But the department doesn't have a dog. Maybe the killer knows that."

"Or wasn't thinking straight," Garrett said. "That fits with panicked. I'd say that might be more likely."

"Maybe the killer didn't think Fawn would be missed," Regina said.

"I have a hard time with that one," Creed said. "Everyone in town knows Fawn and Lacey are tight. And Fawn has a ton of friends at the hospital."

"So, maybe it was someone who stumbled on the place and decided to help themselves. Only Fawn caught him, and he killed her."

"That would fit with the panic burial," Creed said, "but the house was untouched." At least, it had appeared to be. He called Lacey. "Hey," he said, when she answered. "Can you check and see if you notice anything missing, like jewelry or silver or—I don't know—whatever?"

"You think Fawn was killed by an intruder—she caught him, he killed her and hid her body?"

"That's a theory."

"The only thing that I've noticed out of the ordinary was the messy clothing in the drawers. Let me look around and I'll shoot you a text if I find anything else that looks off."

"Thanks."

He hung up and turned back to the scene. "You know, from here, you have a really good view of the house, too. The back of it, anyway. With some binoculars, you could even see inside, if there weren't sheets over the windows."

"You think someone's been watching the place?" Ben asked.

"No idea. Just making an observation." But the thought made him uneasy.

"But why shoot at you?"

"At first, I thought it was a hunter who needed some extra target practice, but now…" He pursed his lips. "I don't know. Even I can see the shed with no trouble.

Whoever was shooting had to see there were people there."

"Then why shoot?"

"Maybe to get us away from the shed? Keep us from getting too close to Fawn's body?"

Regina nodded. "Could be either...or neither. Let's check out the shed just to be thorough."

FIVE

Lacey lay on Fawn's bed and stared at the ceiling. She'd done a cursory walk through the house and hadn't noticed a thing missing. The silver was all there, Fawn's jewelry box was untouched and the smart TV still sat on its stand in the corner of the den. She'd let Creed know, then collapsed onto the bed.

She never did get around to calling Jessica. Instead, she'd dialed her mother's number and had just gotten off the phone with her. Her mother had still been crying when they'd hung up. Lacey's tears had been retriggered, of course, and now the box of tissues was empty on the floor. She needed to get up, but her sinuses were clogged, her head pounded and moving required effort.

She definitely needed to move, but numbness nailed her to the mattress. Scarlett lay at her feet, lifting her head every so often as though checking on her.

Lacey slid her gaze to the dresser. The disarray of the drawers still bothered her. Fawn would never leave her clothes like that. So, why were they *like that*?

Her phone rang. Creed again. Answering his call was the only thing that could inspire her to move at the moment. She snagged the device from the end table. "Hi."

"Do we have permission to search this outbuilding? The shed where we found Hank?"

"Of course." She sat up, her lethargy fleeing. "Why?"

"We're speculating, that's all. Wondering if the shooter was trying to distract us away from the shed. And while we have no proof of that, we're trying to cover all bases."

"I understand. You can search it. Just break the lock. Whatever you need to do."

"Thanks. Be thinking about people who know Fawn. We're going to need to talk to them."

"I've already made a mental list, but I'll write them down."

"I should have figured. Stay strong, Lacey," he said, his voice low. "We're going to find out who did this."

Her heart lightened a fraction. She loved that he included her in that statement. "I know. It won't bring Fawn back, but she deserves justice." She paused. "I *need* her to have justice."

"One step at a time. I'll let you know if we find anything."

"Thanks, Creed."

She hung up and swung her feet to the floor. Scarlett watched from her spot on the bed. "You can stay here," Lacey said. "I'm just going to start a more thorough search of the house."

Lacey went to Fawn's closet and opened the door. She closed her eyes and breathed in the scent of her sister. A subtle hint of her musk perfume and strawberry shampoo. Tears wanted to flow once more. "Stop it," she whispered. "Focus."

For the next two hours, she went through the closet, working her way through all of the pockets. And there were a lot. Fawn loved clothes and had a good eye for style. One would never guess she frequented thrift stores and yard sales to dress herself.

In the end, the search produced two tubes of lip balm and almost six dollars in change. And a note scribbled on hospital letterhead to call Miranda Glenn. Below the reminder were several names. Derrik Jones, Robert Owen, Selena Hernandez. She sent a picture of the paper to Creed via text, then tapped the message: Found this in one of Fawn's pockets. I have no idea who these people are, but maybe you can figure it out.

Good job. Worth investigating.

Her eyes landed on the old childhood photo albums stacked against the back wall of the closet, and she sank to the floor to grab the top one. She flipped through it, the memories flooding her. As much as her father had hurt their family by his actions, they'd had some good times before it all came crashing down, she had to admit. Times that had been buried in the tiniest corner of her mind and mostly forgotten.

Now they surged to the surface, bringing her to tears once more. Beach trips, mountain camping adventures with just the four of them, theme parks and more. She slammed the book closed and shut her burning eyes. "God, I don't know if I can do this," she said out loud. "I need Your strength because mine is about gone." She checked her phone to find she'd missed a text from Creed. He'd sent it thirty minutes ago.

Nothing in the shed. Heading to the morgue to speak with Zeb. No need for you to come, even though I know that's going to be your first thought. He hasn't done the autopsy yet, of course, but I thought if I showed up, he might stop and fill me in on anything he might have found in his initial examination. I'll be in touch.

With another prayer for answers, she slipped out of the closet to find the house pitch-dark. The only light came from the closet. She turned it off, not needing it. She knew this house like the back of her hand—minus the changes in the kitchen. Scarlett waited at the bedroom door, ears cocked. Lacey went to the dog and placed a hand on her head. "What is it, girl?"

Scarlett spared her a quick glance before she walked out of the bedroom and down the hall to the kitchen. Goose bumps pebbled Lacey's arms and she shivered. Scarlett went to the door and barked once. Her signal that she needed out. After Lacey stopped at the thermostat to bump it up a degree, she flipped on the small table lamp next to the back door.

As soon as Lacey opened the door, Scarlett darted straight to the bushes along the side of the house. The fence would keep her from wandering too far.

Lacey scanned the property, hunching her shoulders against the chill. She'd forgotten how dark it was here in the middle of nowhere, and she didn't like it any more now than she had as a kid. Scarlett barked, ears pricked, hackles raised, and Lacey's chills multiplied. "Scarlett! Come."

The dog backed up, ears twitching, reluctant to obey, but trained well enough that she would anyway. "Scarlett, come."

Scarlett whirled and raced to Lacey. Once they were both inside, Lacey shut and locked the door, her mind racing. Was someone out there? Like the person who'd shot at them? She grabbed her phone and called Creed.

He answered on the first ring. "Hey, I can't talk right now. Can I call you back in a few?"

"Um...yeah. That's fine."

A pause. "Everything okay?"

"I'm not sure." She checked her weapon.

"Scarlett was acting weird. I think some-one may be snooping around outside."

"Okay, stay put. I'm on the way."

"No, do what you have to do. I'm going to take Scarlett and kind of scout around the area." Having part of the yard fenced didn't mean someone couldn't have slipped through the gate.

"Look, I know you're a cop and very ca-pable, but even cops need help sometimes. So just don't take any chances."

She heard the words he didn't say. *Don't do anything stupid.* He was right. She didn't like it, but... "Okay. Fine. Will you send someone?"

"Already on it."

"Let them know I'll have my gun, please."

"Of course."

She hung up and went to each window in the house, finding them all locked and secure. While the house still needed to be better insulated, one of the first things Fawn had done was replace the old drafty windows. Too bad she hadn't installed an alarm system.

Scarlett pushed her nose into Lacey's hand. "It's all right, girl. I may just be a little paranoid." Which was understandable, of course.

For the next few minutes, she paced from one end of the dark house to the other, peering out the window and beginning to regret her call to Creed. Keeping the lights off inside should have given her a bit of an advantage to see if anyone was lurking outside, but nothing set her internal alarms off. She looked at Scarlett. "If all of this stress is over a rabbit, we're going to have a serious chat."

Scarlett yawned and settled on her bed, lowering her snout between her paws.

Which made Lacey feel a lot better— and a little like the boy who cried wolf. She made her way to the front door and looked out just in time to see a police cruiser pulled to the top of the U-shaped drive. Regina climbed out, hand on her weapon. Lacey opened the door and stepped out onto the front porch. "Sorry. I think I'm overreacting."

"Overreacting how?"

"I thought someone was lurking around the house. In the bushes. Scarlett was acting weird, and after getting shot at today—" She shrugged. "Now I'm feeling kind of silly."

"Nothing to feel silly about. Getting shot at is kind of terrifying."

"No kidding." Another cruiser turned into her drive and Lacey bit off a groan. After all, she was the one who'd made the call. "Creed, too? Thought he was headed to the morgue."

"He called me and said to get over here and that he was headed here, too. Said the morgue could wait."

Creed parked behind Regina and stepped out of his car. "Lacey? You okay?"

"I'm fine. I was telling Regina I think I overreacted." Heat climbed into her cheeks, and she was thankful she was in the shadows of the porch light. If he thought she was incompetent, he might rethink his offer to join the force. Which shouldn't matter since she couldn't investigate Fawn's case.

And she was leaving as soon as they found Fawn's murderer and set up the K-9 unit for Creed. For some reason, she had to remind herself of that.

He flipped on a flashlight he held in his left hand. "Why don't we find out? Want to help clear the area?"

At least he hadn't told her to go back inside but was treating her as a fellow officer. "Gladly."

"Then lead the way."

She pulled her weapon—just in case she wasn't overreacting—and started for the bushes Scarlett had been so interested in.

Creed followed Lacey while Regina went in the opposite direction, stating she'd radio if she found something. In the meantime, he lit the way for Lacey. She approached, caution in her stance. "This is stupid," she muttered. "If someone *was* here, he's not anymore."

But he noticed she didn't lower her

guard. Every inch the professional, she cleared the bush, then the next and the next, until she finally lowered her weapon and turned to him. "Nothing."

Something on the ground caught his eye. "Maybe not nothing."

"What do you mean?"

Creed knelt and shone the light. "It's a pen with the hospital's logo on it."

"Well, Fawn worked there, so that's not so odd. The fact that it's out here kind of is, though."

He shook his head. "Fawn's probably been dead for a few days. This pen is clean, for the most part. A little dirt to brush off, but definitely not one that's been out here long." He stood and clicked the radio on his shoulder. "Regina? You find anything?"

"Found some trash in one area that's pretty well hidden on the other side of the fence, but is up the hill far enough that it has a clear view of the house. Food wrappers, water bottles and beer cans, that kind of thing. Everything was in a plastic grocery bag and tied off. Looks to me like it was something teenagers might have done, not a shooter."

"Well, bag it all and we'll send it to the lab. Who knows what we'll get?"

"Copy that."

"And can you bring me an evidence bag?"

"You found something?"

"Maybe."

Seconds later, Regina handed him the bag and a pair of gloves. Once he had the gloves on, he snagged the pen and slipped it into the bag. Regina sealed and labeled it. "Thanks," he told her.

"Sure thing. One other thing of note that makes me think Scarlett may have heard someone. The fence was unlatched. And since you can only lock or unlock it from the inside..."

Lacey sucked in an audible breath. "Right. Good to know. I'll buy a lock for it ASAP."

"Good idea." She waved the evidence bag. "If y'all are okay, I'm going to get this back and stored until we can get it sent off first thing in the morning."

"I think we'll be fine. If you'll take care of that, I'll hang out with Lacey a bit longer."

Regina nodded and headed for her cruiser while Lacey stood glaring at the bush, hands on her hips. Then she sighed and turned to face him. "You want to come in for a few minutes? I need something to drink. I'm sure you could use something, too."

"Sounds good."

"Coffee, water or tea?"

"Coffee."

While she popped the pod in the Keurig, he found the cream and sugar. Scarlett watched them from her spot on the floor. "She likes to be around people, doesn't she?"

Lacey shot the dog a fond smile. "Yeah, she definitely doesn't like being left alone too long."

The Keurig gurgled its "I'm finished" noise, and Lacey handed him his steaming mug half-full. He caught her eye. She remembered. Before the eye contact got awkward, he added enough milk to turn the java a light brown and topped it off with a tablespoon of sugar. "Why don't you just drink the milk?" she asked.

He grinned. "You never did understand a good cup of coffee."

"Coffee-flavored milk." She rolled her eyes, and his heart cramped at the banter. He'd been a frequent Saturday morning visitor and coffee consumer in this very room. Shoving the memories aside, he waited while she made her cup of coffee—and left it black. He shuddered and followed her to take a seat at the kitchen table.

"You know, this is a perfect property to raise dogs on."

She narrowed her eyes at him, and he wondered if he'd overstepped. Before he could apologize, she nodded. "It really is, but I have a place."

"Who's taking care of your dogs while you're here?"

"There are only three dogs at the moment, and they'll all be going to their new homes in less than a month. For now, a couple of volunteers and my part-time person are stopping by several times a day to check on them, feed them and so on. They're good people." She sipped her coffee. "Interestingly enough, one of my volunteers is the owner of the property I've been renting for the past few years."

"Renting? You didn't buy something?"

"No."

"Why not?"

She shrugged. "I don't know. I meant to, of course, once I got to know the area, but I just never got around to it. I stayed so busy with the department and business was booming…" Another small lift of her shoulders. "Before I knew it, the years had passed and the place was…comfortable."

But she didn't say *home*. Now, *that* was interesting.

She glanced at the window again. "You think there really was someone out there?"

she asked. "And that someone dropped the pen?"

He let her change the subject. "It's impossible to know for sure, but I think we need to err on the side of caution. Especially after today. Until we know who or what that shooter was aiming at, it's best to watch your back."

"They were shooting at us. I'm not buying the errant-bullets idea."

After a pause, he said, "Yeah, I think so, too." He shook his head. "But most people who own weapons around here are proficient with them. Meaning, they hit what they aim at. If the shooter wanted to hit one of us, I think he would have."

"Maybe. You think it was a warning?"

"I'm hoping it was." He shook his head again. "The only person who knows for sure is the one who pulled the trigger." She covered a yawn and Creed frowned. "Why don't you go get some rest? I'll stay here and keep an eye on things."

She hesitated, like she was debating whether or not to take him up on it, then nodded. "I'll sleep better knowing you're here." More hesitation. "What's the plan for in the morning?"

"I talk to people who knew Fawn. Try to get a picture of her last couple of days and who saw her last. That kind of thing."

"I spoke to Katherine O'Ryan right before we started looking for Hank. She said she saw Fawn at the hospital last week— probably right before she was killed—and said she looked rough, like she'd been sick or something."

"But she wasn't sick?"

"Not that I know of. She never said."

"I'll talk to Katherine again."

"I want to help."

"You can't."

"Not officially, I know. We've already covered that. But I want to talk to people, too. Unofficially. Surely, there's no law against a sister talking to her murdered sister's friends."

"No, there's no law." He massaged his temples. "Let's discuss it in the morning. Why don't you try to get some rest?"

"Okay." She paused. "Thanks, Creed."

Her whisper reached him and touched something deep in his heart. Something he'd thought he'd managed to purge after she'd walked away from him. He let his gaze linger on her face, then cleared his throat. "Of course. Good night."

She clicked to Scarlett and the two of them disappeared down the hall.

Creed lowered his coffee cup to the coaster, refusing to acknowledge that he could possibly still be attracted to the woman who'd stomped all over his heart. He focused on the events of earlier and admitted she was right.

Someone *had* shot at them. That fact continued to rattle around in his tired brain. One shot might have been an accident, but two? When they were standing there in plain sight? He was going to have to go on the assumption that someone had been aiming at them with the intention of killing—and the fact that the shooter hadn't cared that a child might get caught in the cross fire.

So, who did he know in this town that he'd grown up in with the ability to commit cold-blooded murder?

SIX

Lacey had tossed and turned enough to send the comforter to the floor and Scarlett leaping down after it to escape her restless mistress. But, Lacey realized with some shock, she'd slept a few hours.

Low voices from the kitchen reached her and she quickly showered and dressed. She rubbed Scarlett's ears. "Come on, girl. Time for you to go out and for me to get a status update on Fawn's case." If there was one.

When she stepped into the kitchen, Regina and Creed had a newspaper and several pictures spread out on the table in front of them, empty mugs pushed to the side. They looked up at her entrance. "Good morning," Lacey said.

"Good morning to you, too," Creed drawled. "You get some sleep?"

"A bit." She let Scarlett out into the backyard, then looked at Regina. "What brings you here?"

"Creed and I have been taking turns sleeping and keeping watch."

"That's over and above. Thank you."

"Happy to do it."

"What are you looking at?"

Creed passed her the newspaper. A picture of her and Scarlett was on the front page. The headline read K-9 Finds Body of Missing Doctor.

Lacey shuddered and shoved the paper away. "Ugh."

Creed covered her hand with his. "I'm sorry. I thought about hiding it, but—"

"There's no point in that."

"I know."

He set the paper aside and Regina pointed to the other pictures laid out. "They're photos of your property taken by a drone. We believe that the shooter wanted to keep us away from something."

"Like what?"

"Finding Fawn's body is the first thought that comes to mind," Creed said, "but we thought looking at the property from a different angle might give us some new information, reveal something on the property that sparked a reason for the shooting."

"And does it?"

"Not really."

"Oh."

"Yeah. Sorry. We just keep circling back to the shooter not wanting us near Fawn's body." He sighed. "It was a good idea." He pulled one of the pictures toward him. "And actually—" he pointed "—here is where the shooter picked for his hiding spot. We knew it was a good one, but looking at it from above, it's downright genius."

"I see what you mean," Lacey said, her voice low. "He's got a view of the house—even the fenced-in spot, the area where we found Fawn, the shed...everything. And there—" She pointed. "A path straight back to here that leads to the road. There's a fence there, but it wouldn't be any trouble to go over it."

"And have a car waiting right there for a quick getaway."

"But what were they doing up there?" Lacey asked. "And with a long-range rifle? No one would know we were going to be searching there."

"Or they were *afraid* the search might extend that far and went to wait and see."

Lacey nodded. "Of course. But how did they get away so easily? Officers were all over that area." Whenever anyone went missing, law enforcement sent officers to neighboring towns to help search. "Why didn't they see a vehicle or something?"

"They may have," Creed said, "and simply mistaken it for a volunteer's."

True. She sighed. Scarlett barked at the door. Lacey let her in, and she went to the bowls at the end of the cabinet. "I guess you're ready to eat, huh?"

Regina stood. "I need to go give my sister a break. She's been with Mom all night." Fawn had told her that Regina's mother was in the late stages of dementia.

"I'm so sorry about your mom."

"Thanks." She walked toward the door. "I'll be back on shift later this evening. If I learn anything before then, I'll let you know."

"Thanks, Reg," Creed said.

She left, and Lacey filled the bowls with food and water, then scratched Scarlett's floppy ears. The dog sighed her contentment. "Why don't we go into town and start asking questions?" Lacey said. "I'll be ready when Scarlett's finished eating."

He nodded. "I'll drive, if that's all right with you."

"Fine with me. Do you mind if Scarlett comes? She'll be fine in the back seat. I have a seat-belt harness for her."

"Don't mind at all. Who do you want to start with?"

"Miranda Glenn. She and Fawn were close friends. If anyone knows what was going on with Fawn, it's her."

He nodded. "She has a new baby, so I

feel like she's probably at home, but I'll call her on the way to make sure."

After Scarlett finished her last bite of food, Lacey snagged her lead and they followed Creed out to his cruiser. Lacey hooked Scarlett into the harness, then climbed into the passenger seat to fasten her own seat belt. Her stomach twisted at the thought of the upcoming questions she was going to have to ask people who'd known her all her life. The people who'd turned their noses up at her when her father went to prison. And one man in particular who'd screamed at her in the cafeteria of her high school.

Tucker Glenn, one of the lawyers of the only law firm in town. Miranda's husband had not been happy when he'd learned who was responsible for his father's sudden financial crisis. He'd gone ballistic, and she and Fawn had been his targets. She closed her eyes on the image and swallowed the nausea that rose each time she thought of that day he—

"You okay?"

Creed's question pulled her from the past. She sighed. "No, but I know, in time, I will be."

Creed cranked the SUV and backed out of her drive. Miranda and Tucker Glenn lived in a sprawling home just outside of town. Close enough for convenience, but with the illusion that they were in the middle of nowhere. Fawn had mentioned Tucker and Miranda had purchased the place three years ago. Lacey had never been inside the home she'd admired from afar as a youth, but Fawn had been a regular visitor after Miranda and Tucker became the new owners.

Creed called Miranda and got permission to stop by, but Lacey noticed he hadn't mentioned she was with him. They rode in not-quite-comfortable silence for a few minutes. Then he said, "I owe you an apology."

She blinked. "Why?"

"For refusing to tell you goodbye when you left."

She fell silent. "That really hurt," she finally said.

"I know."

"But I know I hurt you, too."

"You did." He sighed. "We hurt each other. We were young and stupid and immature. It's probably a good thing we went our separate ways. Not the way we did it, of course, but..." He shrugged. "It gave us some time to grow up."

She twisted her hands together in her lap. "Yes. I agree with that."

"For a long time after you left, I was angry. Seething. Hurting. And then something happened."

"What?"

He shot her a small smile. "I started to heal."

"Oh."

"And I...forgave." He lowered his eyes, then lifted them to meet hers, the softness there making her heart hitch. "After about a year," he said, "I was tired of carrying that load of anger around and decided the only way to move on was to let it go."

She swallowed. "I'm glad." But he still hadn't tried to get in touch with her. To clear the air.

"I know what you're thinking," he said. "Once I'd let go of the hurt, I had a burning need for closure, to make things right, but I was—"

"Afraid?" She clamped her lips together. Would she never stop interrupting the man?

He cleared his throat. "*Unsure* of my reception should I reach out to you." He paused. "Okay, yes, *afraid* is probably accurate."

Most likely, she would have hung up on him or slammed the door in his face. After his massive rejection, the initial pain had morphed into a raging anger that she'd been unable to let go of for a long time. A fact she was definitely not proud of. "At that point in time," she said, "you were wise to keep your distance."

He nodded. "I'd talked to Fawn—"

"You did? She never said." She grimaced. She'd interrupted him. Again. "Sorry."

"I finally convinced her to listen to me." He rubbed a hand over his mouth and sighed. "I asked her how you were doing and if you still hated me."

"I never hated you." Much.

"Fawn talked about you a lot. She showed me pictures with your dogs and how happy you were." He shook his head and kept his gaze on the road. "I couldn't call you after seeing that. My need for closure was just that—*mine*. Fawn made it clear that you'd moved on and contact with me would be an unwelcome disruption."

Lacey's jaw dropped. Literally. When she could speak, she snapped her mouth shut while she struggled for words. "She never said," she finally croaked out. "She never said a word to me about that."

He nodded. "I asked her not to." His gaze met hers once more. "But I want to know something."

"What?"

He pulled to the curb in front of the Glenns' home. When he cut the engine, he didn't move to get out, but looked at her. "Are you still holding on to the past anger and hurt?"

"No." She wasn't, was she? "But don't ask me for a specific moment in time when I made the conscious decision to move on. I buried myself in work, stayed busy day and night. I'd fall into bed on the few hours I took off and sleep like the dead. At some point, the pain faded, but my work habits didn't." She shot him a rueful smile. "I became known as the one who'd take the extra shift or train 'just one more' dog. The only time I took off work was when Fawn came to visit."

"But you never once came to visit her."

"No."

"Why?"

She gave a silent mental groan but refused to lie to him. "There were a lot of reasons, but mostly because I didn't want to run into you."

The words shouldn't have carried as much punch as they did, but they struck a raw nerve and Creed flinched.

"So," she said, "maybe I wasn't quite as over everything as I liked to think." Her words were low, almost a whisper.

Okay, that helped ease the pain a bit.

"Throughout the first couple of years," she said, "I picked up the phone many times to call you, but then stopped. I told myself the ball was in your court. I'd apologized, asked you to talk, and you'd opted not to. The fact that I never heard from you seemed to indicate you hadn't changed your mind, so I think I just... gave up. Convinced myself you'd never forgive me."

"I'm sorry, Lacey." His husky voice vibrated between them. "I really am."

She gazed at him, her eyes shiny with unshed tears, but she nodded. "I am, too."

"So..." He held out a hand. "Friends?"

"Yeah." She clasped his fingers and her soft touch sent shivers through him. Just like old times. He smiled and she squeezed. "Friends."

He let go of her hand and immediately wanted to grab it back, rewind and tell her he still wanted more than friendship, but for now, they had work to do. And then she'd go home. So…friends it would have to be. For now—and probably forever.

Lacey unhooked Scarlett from her harness and the dog jumped down to shake herself. Then she looked at Lacey as though asking, "What now?"

Creed laughed. "She's got some expressions, doesn't she?"

"It's funny, isn't it," Lacey said. "I can usually figure out what she's thinking."

"Yeah, you were always good at being able to read anything that breathed," he said. Especially him. He remembered the times they communicated with a simple look, then cleared his throat and let Lacey and Scarlett lead the way up the steps to the door. He stayed close behind her, protecting her from anyone who might decide to take another shot at her. Then again, if the shooter had simply been trying to distract them from finding Fawn's body, the reason to shoot at them no longer existed.

But…no need to take any chances.

Lacey knocked. A firm rap that would get someone's attention inside, but hopefully soft enough not to startle a sleeping newborn.

Footsteps sounded from inside and then the door opened. Miranda held her baby in the crook of her left arm. When her gaze landed on him, she frowned. When she saw his companion, she gasped. "Lacey Lee Jefferson? Are you kidding me?"

"Hi, Miranda. Just Lacey, please."

She eyed Creed. "You didn't say anything about bringing Lacey."

"Sorry. Is it okay?" He'd simply told her he needed to talk to her about a few things, but had been intentionally vague.

"Of course. But what's going on?"

"I wanted to ask you some questions about Fawn," Lacey said.

"Fawn?" Miranda shifted the sleeping infant to her shoulder and backed up. "Um…okay, but can you leave the dog outside? I'm not a fan."

Lacey raised a brow, then glanced at Creed. "I'll just go put her back in the car."

"I'm sorry," Miranda said, "but I don't want the dog around the baby and...dogs make me nervous."

"Of course."

"While you do that, I'm going to go answer my phone. I can hear it ringing."

She walked away and Creed unlocked the car. Lacey ordered Scarlett back into her seat, then scratched the dog's ears. "Stay here, girl. You'll be fine for a few minutes."

The dog heaved a sigh and lay down across the seat to settle her nose between her paws.

Lacey rejoined Creed on the porch.

"She doesn't seem happy about being left behind," he said.

"She's not, but she'll be okay." She glanced at him. "And don't think I make a habit of leaving her in a vehicle—I'm only doing so because the weather is cold and we're only going to be a few minutes. If it was summer, I'd never do it."

"It never crossed my mind that you would."

Miranda appeared and opened the storm door once more. "Come on in." She kept her voice soft, almost a whisper.

Lacey and Creed stepped into her foyer.

"Let me just put TJ down." Miranda walked to the bassinet located next to the recliner, lowered the baby into it, then gestured for them to have a seat on the couch. "He's a good baby. Sleeps through just about everything—except at night, of course."

"TJ?" Lacey asked when she was settled.

"Tucker Junior." Miranda smiled. Beamed, actually. "Tucker's always wanted a son named after him. Now he has one."

"Congratulations," Creed said.

"Thank you." She continued to smile as though the baby had turned on a light inside of her. "We have a lot of plans for this little one. Tucker can't wait for TJ to be old enough to start grooming him for a successful law career. He's already designed the logo for the office. Glenn and Glenn, Attorneys at Law."

Creed blinked. "What if TJ doesn't want to be a lawyer?"

Miranda laughed and flashed a tight smile. "Of course he will. Why wouldn't he?"

Creed had nothing to say that wouldn't sound harsh, so he just bit his tongue and nodded.

"You look amazing," Lacey said, breaking into the awkward moment. "Clean hair, makeup and dressed. You're a superwoman."

Miranda chuckled. "For the first time in over a week. When my mother was here helping, it was fairly easy. She never wanted to let go of him. But this morning, I told Tucker he wasn't going to work—and definitely not meeting up with his hunting buddies—until I had a shower and felt human again." She sat in the recliner and folded her hands in her lap. "What did you want to ask me about in regard to Fawn?"

"Have you seen her lately?"

Miranda frowned. "No, but that's not

unusual. She stays so busy with the hospital these days that we can go several days without talking and weeks without getting together. We do text often, though."

"When's the last time you talked to her in person?" Creed asked.

Miranda tapped her lips. "Two weeks ago? No, that's not right. Last week? Monday, maybe?" She sighed. "I'm sorry. Days are blending together right now. She came by to see TJ shortly after he was born and then said she was going to be busy playing catch-up at work—she was involved in some kind of research project—and it might be a while before she could get back. I told her I had six weeks—then I was meeting her at the gym as soon as I was cleared. She laughed and told me to take advantage of my 'enforced exercise downtime.'" The woman shrugged. "That was on the day she came to see TJ, which was the day after he was born, so, yes, about two weeks ago. I'm sorry. I haven't really thought about it, to be honest. Having a newborn is a lot more work than I ever imagined, and I don't have time to think, much less process time." She shot a loving look at the baby. "But I wouldn't change a thing."

"So, you saw her during the three months she took off work?"

Miranda frowned. "No, I didn't. I just saw her after TJ was born. We texted quite a bit while she was on her sabbatical—wherever that was—but I didn't see her. I don't think anyone did."

"Did she say where she was?"

"No." She pursed her lips. "And I could tell she didn't want to talk about it, so I didn't press her. I figured she'd tell me in her own time."

"I'm sure." Creed leaned forward. "Do you know if Fawn was having any trouble with anyone in town or at work?"

"Trouble?" Miranda raised a brow. "Not that I can think of right off. Why?"

Lacey met Creed's gaze, then flicked back to Miranda. "You haven't heard?" Lacey asked.

Miranda's expression changed. She

frowned again, worry flickering in her eyes. "No. Heard what? Why are you asking all these questions about Fawn?"

SEVEN

"Fawn's dead, Miranda," Creed said softly.

Miranda blinked at him. "What? No, she's not."

"I just assumed you saw the paper."

"I don't do anything but take care of a baby and try to sleep when he does, so no, I haven't seen the paper. Please, what are you talking about? How can she be dead?"

"We found her...body—" Lacey could barely say the word without choking "—yesterday. I'd been trying to get in touch with her, and when I couldn't—and I couldn't get you on the phone or a straight answer from her work—I came to find her."

Miranda's hand lifted as though in slow motion to cover her mouth while her eyes filled with tears. "What? No. That's not possible. I just…saw her. Talked to her. Didn't I?"

"Like you said, you've probably lost all sense of time." Lacey paused. "Why didn't you call me back? I left you a couple of messages."

"I… I didn't get any messages." She pushed her hands into her hair, then smoothed it down and shook her head. "I'm just not on my phone much these days. Half the time I can't even find it. Did you try to get Tucker?"

"No. I didn't…have his number."

Creed shot her a quick look, and she avoided his eyes. She could have gotten the number. She'd just wanted to try every other avenue first. Fawn hadn't really cared for Tucker ever since he'd yelled at her and Lacey about their father stealing his family's money. And she'd thought Miranda deserved better. Lacey agreed. But, for the sake of keeping the peace and seeing her friend, Fawn and Tucker had learned to tolerate each other—although Fawn said he would throw in a snide comment about their father whenever he got the chance. Fawn ignored him.

By the time Lacey had been ready to break down and call Tucker about Fawn's lack of communication, she'd already known she was going to have to come back to Timber Creek to find Fawn herself.

The baby stirred and let out a soft cry. Miranda jumped to her feet and picked him up. "I need to feed him."

Creed stood. "We'll get out of your way, then. Do you mind calling if you think of anything else?"

"Of course I will."

"Thanks, Miranda," Lacey said. "One more question. What gym did you and Fawn go to? I never heard her mention a specific one, just that she was trying to be good about working out on a regular basis in order to keep her stress levels under control."

"It's Mike's Gym on South Main Street."

"Thanks." Lacey noted the woman's tenderness in holding the baby, and a pang of longing shot through her. She'd always wanted children—and had thought she and Creed would be raising them together. When they went their separate ways, that dream had withered and died. She forced a smile. "It was good to see you." Strangely, she meant the words.

"You, too, Lacey."

Once they were back in Creed's cruiser—and Scarlett had an appropriate belly rub that earned her forgiveness for being left behind—he looked at her. "Bit of a controlling person, isn't she? Miranda, not Scarlett."

"Ha. You think? I wonder what she'll do if TJ decides to be an artist instead of a lawyer."

"I'm not sure I want to be around to see that reaction." He paused. "You okay?"

She shot him a small smile. "You don't have to keep asking me that, you know."

"Okay, sorry."

"And you don't have to apologize for asking either. But thanks for being concerned." A sigh slipped from her. "I'm okay at the moment. Being proactive in searching for Fawn's killer—albeit unofficially—helps." She paused. "I was worried how Miranda would feel seeing me on her doorstep."

"She seemed a little hesitant at first, but warmed up pretty quickly."

"I guess Tucker's dislike of me doesn't extend to Miranda."

Creed had been there for part of Tucker's verbal tirade in the lunchroom at the high school her senior year. Fawn had come to eat lunch with her, and Tucker had walked in and let them have it. Fawn had yelled back and told him off, but Lacey had sat there, feeling the wound of each word Tucker hurled.

Creed had arrived late to lunch and walked in on the tail end of everything. Lacey had managed to hold on to her tears until the school resource officer hauled Tucker away from the area. She'd even managed to convince Fawn she was fine until her sister left. Then Creed had ushered Lacey out to his car and held her while she'd wept.

His hand covered hers, pulling her out of the memory, and she could tell he'd been remembering that shared moment from their past, as well. "You were always there for me, Creed," she said. "You always had my back." Until he hadn't. She cleared her throat. "All right, what's next?"

"The hospital."

"I've talked to everyone Fawn ever mentioned from her work."

"What about her supervisor?"

"Yes, him, too. He was less than helpful, just sounded like he had more on his plate than he knew what to do with."

"Okay, I've done the paperwork for the subpoena on her credit cards, her bank stuff and her phone records. I'm just waiting on that to come back."

Lacey pressed her palms to her eyes. "If I knew where to find that stuff, I'd just give it to you. Then again, she may have paid all of her bills and stuff online, and I'm not sure I can figure out the passwords."

"It's okay. It shouldn't be much longer."

Lacey paused. "Come to think of it, I don't remember seeing her laptop anywhere. I'll go through her desk when I get home. In the meantime, why don't we head to the gym before we go to the hospital? It's only about a mile from here."

"And not too far from the café," he said. "Want to grab a bite to eat afterward?"

"Sure."

When Creed pulled into the parking lot of the gym, Lacey swallowed a surge of emotion. Fawn had always been big into working out and staying in shape, but once she'd started at the hospital, she'd gotten out of the habit of going. About a year ago, she'd told Lacey about her renewed efforts in the gym. "You should come home and join me."

"I don't need a gym. I have the dogs."

"You just don't want to come home."

"Timber Creek's not my home anymore."

"I know," Fawn had said, "but a sister can hope, can't she?"

"Lacey? Hello? You there?"

Creed waved a hand in front of her eyes

and she blinked. Heat crept into her cheeks. "I'm sorry. I was just thinking that Fawn wanted me to come home. Move home for good. I balked, of course. Wouldn't even consider it." She frowned. "Maybe if I hadn't been so…selfish…she'd still be alive."

"What do you mean? Give up the job you love and move back to a town you hate because your sister asked you to?"

She huffed a short laugh. "Well, when you put it like that…" She paused. "Sounds kind of silly, doesn't it?"

"A little."

"And, I have to admit, coming home hasn't been nearly as traumatic as I thought it would be—discounting Fawn's death." That was about as traumatic as one could get. "I'm just talking about the townspeople. Everyone has been so…nice." Of course, she hadn't run into a whole lot of people yet.

"Welcoming?"

"Yes. Fawn said…"

"Said what?"

"...said I should give the town a second chance, that I'd built it up so much in my head as a horrid place with no one good here." Tears wanted to flow once more. "I wish I'd listened to her," she finally said on a whisper.

"No one blames you or Fawn for what your father did. He's the one who stole money and blamed it on bad investments, not you." She shot him a sideways glance of disbelief and he sighed. "Okay, there may be a few individuals with misplaced anger, but the majority don't."

She nodded. "I think I'm starting to see that." She turned to Scarlett. "Sorry, girl. You have to stay here this time, too."

Scarlett hesitated as though she couldn't believe Lacey was doing this to her again. "You'll be fine. Rest while you can. We could get a call at any time."

The dog tilted her head, realized she wasn't going and dropped onto the seat with a huff. When she turned her head away from Lacey, Lacey bit her lip on a smile and looked at Creed. "Guess she gets an extra-long belly rub when we get back."

He shook his head. "She's not a happy girl."

"She'll be fine."

He followed her into the gym and Lacey made her way to the desk. A young man in his late twenties shot her a dimpled smile. "Hi. Welcome to Mike's. Sheriff Payne, good to see you." He returned his attention to Lacey. "I don't think I've seen you around. What can I do for you?"

Lacey ignored his flirty smile. "Hi, Mike. I'm Lacey Jefferson. Do you know my sister, Fawn?"

"Of course. She's a regular. Or was. I haven't seen her in forever."

"When was the last time she was here?"

"Let me just check the computer." He shook the mouse, clicked a few keys, then looked up. "She was here a little over three months ago."

Lacey shot a look at Creed. "There's that three-month time frame once more."

"Something wrong?" Mike asked.

"She's dead," Creed said. "Someone… murdered her."

"*Murdered* her?" Mike's eyes had gone wide and his jaw swung open. He finally snapped it shut. "But…how? Why?"

Keeping her emotions under control, she gave him the short version. "Now we're working on figuring out the why. And the who. Can you tell us anyone she might have had an issue with?"

"Not an issue bad enough to kill her over." He frowned and shook his head. "No, no one comes to mind. Everyone loved Fawn." He rubbed a hand down his face, then paused. "She has a locker here. Do you want to take a look?"

Lacey raised a brow. "Yes. Absolutely."

"I don't know the combination to her lock."

"I've got bolt cutters in the SUV," Creed said. "Hang tight while I grab them." He left and returned in under a minute. "Where's the locker?"

Mike nodded toward the hallway. "Down there. Women's on the right, men's on the left." He consulted the computer once more. "She paid via a monthly draft for locker number six." He drew in a breath. "Hey, wait a minute. I just thought of someone you might want to talk to."

Creed raised a brow. "Who?"

"Gracie Martin. She's a trainer here. She and Fawn often worked out together. Gracie also works in the membership office. Maybe Fawn talked to her?"

"Is Gracie here now?"

"Yeah. She's in the office. Two doors before you get to the women's locker room."

Lacey hesitated, then held out a hand for the bolt cutters. "I'll take the locker. You take Gracie Martin. Is that all right?"

"Sure." Creed handed her the cutters. "That'll keep us from having to clear out the ladies' locker room so I can be in there."

"Take notes," Lacey told him. "I'm going to want a word-for-word replay. Please?"

"You got it." He followed her down the hall and stopped at the membership office door. Lacey waited until he stepped inside and introduced himself to the young woman at the desk before she pushed into the locker room. Straight ahead were the toilets. To the right were several rows of lockers. Behind the lockers were the showers and the sauna. The place smelled of hair spray, shampoo and sweat.

One of the showers was running, and another woman Lacey had never seen before stood in front of the mirror, drying her hair.

Lacey bypassed her, searched for locker number six and cut the bolt off just as the hair-drying woman finished up. She turned to watch, her eyes wide. "What are you doing?"

"It's okay," Lacey said. "I'm a cop." She pulled her jacket away from the badge she'd clipped on her belt.

"Oh. Okay. For a minute there—"

"Yeah. It's all good."

The woman tossed her brush into her bag, snagged it and headed for the door.

Lacey opened the locker door. Her sister's scent—a mixture of her strawberry shampoo and her light perfume—wafted out to bring the tears to the surface once more. A picture of the two of them was taped to the inside of the door. They stood at the edge of the lake, arms across each other's shoulders, beaming at the camera.

Lacey remembered that day like it was yesterday. Her father had been in good spirits and whisked them away to the lake for a fun afternoon of tubing and swimming. She had no idea where her mother had been, but the good memory of her father was there before she could cut it off.

"Aw, Fawn, that's so you." A picture to remind her of the good times so she wouldn't dwell on the bad. "I wish I was more like you, sis."

The door to the room opened and the woman from the shower exited, but Lacey barely registered that as she forced herself from memory lane to pull the gym bag— the only other item in the locker—from the opening.

She carried it to the bench and unzipped it to reveal the contents. A clean change of clothing consisting of a long-sleeved

T-shirt, leggings, socks and a pair of tennis shoes. She also found shampoo, a towel, hair dryer—and a set of keys. Lacey frowned. That was odd. Why the keys? Seemed like Fawn would have kept them with her. Unless they were a spare set that she wanted to keep in a safe place?

The squeak of a shoe on the tile near the showers caught her attention, and she looked up just as the lights went out.

Lacey stilled, her hand tightening around the material of the bag. "Hello? Someone's in here." Silence. "Can you turn the lights back on, please?"

Nothing.

Then her ears picked up the sound of soft breathing. She curled her fingers around the keys and threaded them through her knuckles. The only light in the area came from the hair dryers mounted on the wall. The built-in "night-light" cut through the shadows in that area while Lacey was in pitch-black darkness.

She grabbed Fawn's bag and headed away from the door she'd entered and aimed herself for the emergency exit. The door that would sound an alarm as soon as she pushed through it.

Just as she reached for the handle, something slammed into her back. The bag dropped from her hand and she let out a sharp cry. Pain raced into her shoulders, and she found herself shoved against the wall, cheek pressed tightly against the unforgiving surface. She couldn't even move the hand that held the keys. "Stop!"

"Go back where you came from or you're going to find yourself as dead as your sister. This is the last warning you'll get."

"Did you shoot at me?" She gasped the question.

"Yeah, and next time I won't miss." He flung her to the ground and pushed out the door.

When the alarm sounded, Creed stood. So did Gracie, the woman who'd promised she had no idea who might have it in for Fawn. "Where's that coming from?" he asked.

"The women's locker room. Someone went out the emergency exit."

"Lacey!" He bolted out of the office and hit the door to the locker room, only to pull up short when he realized the lights were off. "Lacey!"

His shout echoed through the empty area and he beelined toward the exit. He reached the door and raced through it into the back alley. The fading roar of a motorcycle reached him and the alarm abruptly cut off.

"Lacey!"

"I'm here." She rounded the corner at the back of the building, weapon in hand.

"Are you okay?"

"I'm fine, but he got away."

"Who got away?"

"The guy who attacked me in the locker room."

Creed's heart dropped. "*Attacked* you? I need details, please."

"The lights went out. I heard him near the bathroom and bolted for the emergency exit. He caught me and slammed me into the wall." She touched her cheek and he noted the red area.

"Then what?"

"He ran out of the emergency door. I chased him and he jumped on a motorcycle and took off." She pointed to the camera mounted above the door. "We need the footage from that camera."

He nodded. "I'll request it."

He also put a BOLO out on the motorcycle, then turned back to her. "Did you have time to look in Fawn's locker?"

"Yes, but I don't think it's going to tell us much." She paused. "Although, there was a bag with a set of keys in it." She lifted her hand as though surprised to see she still clutched the keys. "I dropped the bag."

"Let's get it and see if you missed anything." Her color was returning and her breathing had evened out. "Feeling better?"

"A lot. He said for me to go back where I came from and that this was the *last* warning I'd get." She met his gaze. "I asked him if he was the shooter. He said he was and next time he wouldn't miss."

"Whoa."

"I know."

"And you didn't get a look at him at all?"

"No." She paused and gave him the once-over. "But he's probably an inch or two taller than you. He was solid. He pressed me up against the wall——" a shudder rippled through her and Creed wanted to get his hands on the guy "——and he didn't have an ounce of fat on him," she said. "He was strong. Very strong." She rubbed her sore arm. "He threw me around like I was a rag doll, and I'm not exactly tiny."

No, she was five feet seven inches and probably in the range of a hundred and forty or fifty pounds. Not exactly rag-doll status.

"But," she said, "I guess that answers one question."

"What?"

"Sounds like Fawn wasn't the victim of some random intruder who killed her and moved on. There's something else going on here."

"I agree." Creed rubbed a hand down

his cheek. "All right, we need to regroup." He thought for a moment. "We're doing the right thing in talking to people here in town, but you need to keep searching the house."

"I know."

He nodded to the keys in her hand. "And I want to know what those go to."

"There are only four. It shouldn't be too hard to figure out what they fit." She held them up. "This one looks like an extra house key." She moved to the next one. "This looks like a key to her mailbox, maybe? I noticed she had a new one with a lock, and this key looks fairly new." She held up the third key. "No idea what this one could be, but this last one is similar to the one that might be a mailbox key."

"Does she have a home office? A desk drawer or a file cabinet?"

"Yes, I saw a desk in her guest room. I'll check and see if there's a lock when I go back. I'll also be looking for any current bank records or credit card statements." She touched her cheek and worked her jaw.

"You need to get checked out at the hospital?"

"Nope. I'm fine. Just sore. Did Gracie tell you anything?"

"Not much. She did say Fawn seemed to have something on her mind. When Gracie asked her about it, she said she had a big decision to make and wasn't sure what to do about it."

"But no details?"

"No. Gracie said she asked, but Fawn brushed her off."

"A big decision," Lacey said slowly. "I have no idea what that could be."

"We'll find out."

"Yes," she said, drawing in a deep breath. "Yes, we will. In the meantime, I know one thing for sure."

He raised a brow. "What's that?"

"From now on, wherever I go, Scarlett does, too."

"I think that's probably wise."

EIGHT

Lacey's phone rang and she snatched it to look at the screen. "It's Katherine."

"Go ahead and take the call while I take care of getting the footage," Creed said.

She nodded and swiped the screen while she followed him back into the gym. "Hello?"

"Hi, Lacey. I'm sorry to bother you, but I heard about Fawn and I'm so sorry."

"Thank you, Katherine. I appreciate it."

"I remembered something and I wasn't sure whether I should repeat it or not, but in light of Fawn's death, I'm going to do something I try never to do."

"What is it?"

"It's a rumor floating around the hospital about Fawn being involved with another doctor."

"Involved? Define *involved*."

"I'm not sure exactly *how* involved, but the rumor implied they were seeing each other. Like dating."

"Fawn never mentioned that to me. Who is he?"

"I don't know. I don't even remember where I heard it from. I don't like gossip and try not to listen to it. However, I have a friend who admired Fawn from a distance. He wanted me to find out if she was dating anyone while he worked up the nerve to ask her out."

"Who?"

"His name is Kevin Garrison. Anyway, I spotted Fawn at the hospital about a year ago and asked her if she was interested in being set up on a blind date. She said no because she was seeing someone. But said to ask her again in a couple of months because she wasn't sure her current relationship was going anywhere."

"But she was definitely seeing someone."

"Yes. She said it was complicated and she was still trying to figure things out."

Complicated. Awesome.

"Did she say what she meant by *complicated*?"

"No," Katherine said, "and I didn't press her for details because we didn't have that kind of friendship. I did offer to listen if she ever wanted to talk about it, but we never spoke of it again after that conversation."

"Okay, thank you. I appreciate you calling."

A hospital page in the background came through the line. "I've got to go."

"I heard. Thank you again." Katherine hung up and Lacey tucked her phone into the back pocket of her pants.

"What was that all about?" Creed asked.

She told him. "Feel like a visit to the hospital to see if we can figure out who this doctor might be?"

He nodded to her cheek. "If you'll let someone check you out."

"I don't need to be checked out, Creed. I'm fine."

"This time."

She sighed. "Right. Well, he achieved his goal. He scared me to death and issued his warning. I guess he'll be watching to see if I leave town or not."

"Which you're not."

She shot him a tight smile. "You know me so well." His eyes darkened, and a flash of longing made her want to reach out to him. To say they could figure out their differences and try again. Instead, she curled her fingers into a hard fist. He looked away and cleared his throat and the moment was gone.

"Also," he said, "you know those three names you found written on the paper from Fawn's pocket?"

"Yes?"

"I just got a text from Regina. She was running them down for me, and they all work at the same hospital in Charlotte, but they're heads of different departments."

She frowned. "Okay. Why would she have their names?"

"I don't know, but I'm going to hazard a guess that Fawn was interviewing for jobs."

"What? No. Fawn loved her job in the ER here. I can't imagine her wanting to leave."

He narrowed his eyes at her. "I hate to say this, Lacey, but it sounds like Fawn was living a very different life than the one she led you to believe."

Lacey scoffed, then fell silent. "But why?" she finally asked.

"That, I can't answer."

She bit her lip and frowned at him. "You think the job was the big decision she had to make? The one she mentioned to Gracie?"

"I'd say that's a real possibility."

Once they were all back in his vehicle, he aimed it toward the hospital. He glanced at her. "Who did you talk to when you called to ask about Fawn?"

"Her supervisor."

"Anyone else?"

"One of Fawn's coworkers, Dr. Jill Holloway, but she said she hadn't seen Fawn since she'd taken her sabbatical. She said she was off the two days Fawn worked before she disappeared." She frowned. "She was also going to check with someone else who was close to Fawn, but by the time I left home to come here, we hadn't connected again. She was one of the first people I'd planned to talk to after you and Miranda, but...well...you know how things played out."

"I do." He pulled into the parking spot reserved for law enforcement and they climbed out of his cruiser. Lacey released Scarlett from the back, buckled her "uniform" around her identifying her as a working dog, and they pushed through the revolving door.

Lacey and Creed walked to the information desk, where Pauline Coulson, a woman in her midsixties who'd taught Lacey's fifth-grade Sunday school class, spoke into a headset. "Transferring you now." When she hung up, she smiled. "Creed, so good to see you." Her gaze slid to Lacey and her smile into an expression of deep sorrow—and not a hint of condemnation. "Lacey Lee Jefferson? Oh, my dear, I'm so sorry to hear about Fawn."

"Thank you." Word had spread. Lacey refused to allow the tears to surface once more. "I'm heartbroken, as you can imagine."

"Indeed. Everyone who knew Fawn has just been shattered by her death. What can I do for you?"

"We're here to speak to Dr. Jill Holloway. She worked with Fawn. Is she here today?" He glanced at Lacey. "Guess we should have checked on that before coming out here."

Mrs. Coulson turned to her computer, and after a few clicks, she looked up. "She is. She's in the emergency department." Her frown deepened the creases in her forehead. "Is there anything I can do?"

"When was the last time you talked to Fawn?" Lacey asked.

"Her first day back from her leave. I was hoping she'd enjoyed her sabbatical, but it didn't look like she had a very good time."

"Why?"

She shrugged. "She was wan and pale. And she seemed sad."

"So not sick?"

"No, she didn't seem sick, just not her usual bubbly self."

"Do you know what she was possibly sad about?"

"I have no idea. She always said hello and we chatted occasionally, but we weren't close."

"Okay, thank you." Lacey noticed the cafeteria to her right and the three lab-coated figures walking into it. "Mrs. Coulson, you have a pretty good view of the cafeteria. Did you notice anyone Fawn ate her meals with? Anyone who stood out to you?" Like a male doctor she could have been involved with? Lacey kept that last thought to herself.

Mrs. Coulson rubbed her chin. "No, can't say I ever thought about it. She'd go in there with a lot of different people from various departments. Sometimes with nurses, other times doctors. Most of the time with Dr. Holloway." She shook her head. "But no one specific person who made an impression on me."

"Thank you, Mrs. Coulson," Creed said. "Appreciate your help."

The woman came around the counter to hug Lacey. "Please let me know if there's anything I can do for you."

Lacey smiled and patted her shoulder. "Thank you." She clicked to Scarlett and headed for the ER before she completely broke down. She didn't have time for tears. Fawn needed her to get her justice.

Creed stepped up beside her on the other side of Scarlett. "Do you know Dr. Holloway?"

"No. Fawn said she was new to town. She's only been here about a year, I think."

They walked to the doors of the ER and Lacey prepared herself to see people she hadn't talked to since she'd left town.

"Why don't you see if Jill can talk to us anytime soon?"

Creed nodded. "Sure." He went to the desk and chatted with a man who looked familiar, but Lacey couldn't place him. When Creed nodded to her, she and Scarlett followed him and the worker through the electronic doors and into the back.

"Come this way," the man said. "You can wait in the conference room. I'll let Dr. Holloway know you're here." His eyes met Lacey's for a brief second, and she blinked at the expression in them. Judgment and disdain.

So, there it was.

Lacey took a seat at the table and Scarlett lay down next to her. "Who was that?" Lacey asked Creed once he was seated across from her.

"Tucker Glenn's brother, James."

"That was *James*? I didn't recognize him, but that explains the look."

"I noticed that, too. I was hoping it went past you."

She raised a brow at him. "If I wasn't

looking for it in every person I come across, then maybe I wouldn't have seen it, but…" She shrugged.

"You look for it."

She pulled in a deep breath and nodded. "I do." She glanced back at him. "It was bad in high school, Creed."

"I knew it was at first," he said, "after your father was arrested. But as time went by, it seemed to get better."

She sighed. "If it did, I couldn't tell. Everywhere I went, I felt like people were watching. Judging. Waiting for me to lift something from their shops, snatch their purse at church or…whatever. I told you about it."

He studied her and then pursed his lips. "Yes. And I apologize again that I didn't take it as seriously as I should have." He leaned forward and clasped her hands. "I really am sorry."

For a brief moment, Lacey allowed herself to enjoy the warmth of his touch, to remember walking hand in hand on the path around the lake, those stolen summer moments that she cherished but couldn't think about too often without the pain of her loss overwhelming her. Before she could answer, the door opened and a woman about Fawn's age stepped into the room. Her eyes were red-rimmed as though she'd been crying and had just managed to get her tears under control. "Hi, I'm Jill Holloway. James said you needed to talk to me."

"Do you have a moment to sit down?" Creed asked.

"A brief one." She slid into the chair at the end of the table and looked at Scarlett. "Beautiful dog. Fawn told me a lot about your K-9 job. She was very proud of you."

"Thank you," Lacey said, ignoring the way her throat wanted to close and the tears threatened to fall. "You and I talked a bit on the phone, but then you were called away to an emergency."

"I remember, but I told you everything I know." She swiped a tissue under her eyes. "Sorry. I'd just heard about her death before James found me. Our supervisor called a quick meeting to let us know. I'm so sorry."

"Thank you. It's been a shock for sure." *Focus, Lacey. Get her justice. Then you can grieve.* "How well did you know her?"

"Really well. We told each other everything." She frowned. "At least, almost everything."

"Then you know where she was those three months that she seems to have dropped off the earth?"

"No. That's what I meant by *almost*." She sniffed. "She said she was taking a leave of absence, but wouldn't tell me where she was going. She texted every so often to let me know she was okay, but other than that, I don't have a clue what she was doing."

"That doesn't sound like Fawn," Lacey said. But then, a lot of things weren't sounding like her sister. At this point, she was starting to wonder if she even knew her. "Another friend of Fawn's said she was seeing someone. A doctor. Do you know who that might have been?"

Jill's eyes widened a fraction. "Um, no. Sorry. I don't know who he is."

"But you knew she was seeing someone." Lacey leaned in. "Come on, Dr. Holloway… Jill… Fawn's dead and someone killed her. When you and I talked on the phone a couple of days ago, she was only missing. But now things are real, and I want to know who killed her. If you know whom she was dating, then, please, tell me. I'm not going to accuse him of anything, but I—" She glanced at Creed. "*We* would like to talk to him."

The woman sighed and looked at her watch. "I don't know who it was. I promise. But yes, it was someone here at the hospital, I think. When we were working the same shift, I'd cover for her every so often so she could meet him."

"Meet him where?"

"I don't know. I asked her once and she said it was better if I didn't know."

Well, that didn't sound good. "Was he married?"

"Honestly, I don't know, but…that was

my first thought, too. I even asked her, and she just said she wasn't ready to talk about it yet."

"Did you know she planned on leaving the hospital?" Creed asked. "That she was interviewing with a hospital in Charlotte?"

Jill frowned. "What? No, she wasn't. What makes you say that?"

He held up his phone. "My deputy Regina just texted and said she'd talked to two of the men. They've confirmed Fawn had interviews with each of them. They were done online."

"When?"

"One was two months ago, and one was three weeks ago."

Jill sat back in her chair and stared at Creed. "She didn't tell me."

"She didn't tell me either," Lacey said. "On the phone, you said there was someone else who could possibly tell me more."

"Dr. Charles Rhodes," she said. "I don't know what he can tell you, but he and Fawn were working together on a new project. I'm not sure of all the details, but part of it was a trial drug to help Alzheimer patients."

"Thank you."

Jill stood. "If I think of anything else, I'll let you know." Tears rose to the surface once more. "I'm so sorry about Fawn."

"Thank you."

And then she was gone, leaving Lacey and Creed looking at each other.

"Dr. Rhodes?" Creed asked.

Lacey rose and gathered Scarlett's leash. "Let's go."

Creed had let Lacey carry that conversation without interrupting because she'd spoken to the doctor already. And he'd wanted to watch Jill's facial expressions and body language. All of which had come across as open and honest, with nothing to hide. None of which was very helpful, except to rule her out in his mind as being a suspect.

On the way down the hall, Creed placed a hand on Lacey's arm and she stopped to look at him. "I need you to back off at this point."

"But, Creed—"

"I'm serious, Lacey. Up to this point, I can explain your presence in the investigation. Fawn and Miranda were friends and it's natural that you would talk to her about Fawn. While the locker at the gym might be a tad harder to justify, it's not impossible. Even talking to Dr. Holloway, Jill, was slightly okay since you'd already spoken with her. But this is a different situation."

She visibly struggled with his words, then finally nodded. "All right. I'll keep my mouth shut and let you do this. Just don't make me sit outside. Please."

He sighed and nodded. "Only if you promise not to interfere in the questioning."

"I promise."

Dr. Rhodes was in a meeting when they arrived at his office, but the administrative assistant told them she thought he would be finished soon and they could wait if they wanted.

They wanted.

Seated on the couch, Creed looked around. "Well, this is nice," he murmured, glancing at the decor.

"He's got an administrative assistant and everything," Lacey said just as softly. "I take it he's not a regular doc."

"No, looks like he's at the top of the food chain."

Scarlett nudged Lacey's hand and she scratched the dog's ears. "Are you bored, girl?"

Creed smiled. "She's been very patient."

"She has a really good temperament. I found her in a local shelter, just sitting behind the fence, staring at me with those big dark eyes. She was one of those rare finds where you know she's just the one you've been looking for."

"Yeah, I know about those kinds of finds." His eyes held hers, and when her cheeks instantly turned pink, he knew she'd gotten the message behind his words.

"You can go in now." The woman behind the desk spoke and Lacey shot to her feet. Creed and Scarlett rose and followed her into Dr. Rhodes's office.

The man had entered through a different door and was already seated behind the mammoth-sized desk. He stood and shook their hands while Creed introduced them. He settled in his chair once more, then gestured for them to have a seat on the couch that faced him. "What can I do for you?"

"I'm sure you've heard about Fawn Jefferson by now. That she was found murdered."

The man swallowed. "Yes. I'd heard."

"I believe you knew her?" Creed asked.

The man paused a fraction, then folded his hands on top of the desk and nodded. "I knew Fawn very well. In a professional capacity, of course, but the more I worked with her, the more I came to appreciate her as a person. As a friend and colleague. She was a brilliant woman. But...why are you asking me about her?"

"Your name was given to me during a routine questioning of one of her friends."

"I see."

"So, do you know of someone she was seeing?" Creed asked. "Dating? Rumor has it that she was involved with another doctor here at the hospital, but she was keeping the relationship secret for whatever reason."

He frowned. "I can't imagine why she'd keep it a secret, unless it would have been a conflict of interest or something. There's no policy that says doctors can't date. There *is* a policy that says you have to sign a statement that you're in a romantic relationship with someone you work with, but I'm not sure how many people actually do it."

"Well, if she was wanting to keep the relationship a secret, she wouldn't fill out a form announcing it," Creed said. "Did she confide in you as to why she was taking off for three months?"

"She didn't. She just said she had some personal issues she needed to take care of, and she'd be in touch. During the three months, she did field some questions about the research she and I were doing in the trial with Alzheimer patients, but other than that, I never heard from her." He blew out a low breath and rubbed his forehead. "I can't believe she's dead."

"That makes two of us," Lacey muttered. Creed wished he could ease the pain so clearly written on her face.

Creed let his gaze roam the office. The man had a plethora of pictures behind him on the credenza. "You have a large family. Looks like you all are very close."

Dr. Rhodes turned a fond eye on the collection. "Yes. We are. My daughter just had her third child a couple of weeks ago." He smiled. "The more the merrier."

"How many children do you have?"

"Three. Ages sixteen, eighteen and twenty-four. I also have three grandchildren. A boy aged four, a girl aged two and the newborn." He nodded to the pictures. "They're my life. I don't know what I'd do if I lost even one of them."

Lacey flinched and Creed covered her hand and squeezed. But one picture in particular caught his eye. "Is that Fawn in one of them?" Creed asked.

The doctor nodded. "Once we started working together, I introduced her to my family and we all fell in love with her. Everyone's going to miss her." He blinked and swiped a hand over his eyes.

"Looks like y'all went hunting together?" Creed pointed to the picture of Fawn holding a rifle. She was flanked by two other women.

"That was a onetime thing for Fawn, but I'm part of a regular group who hunt when we get the chance. My wife and daughter-in-law go occasionally. We invited Fawn along the last time we went." His lips curved upward. "She hated it. Said it was a one and done for her."

"No, she could never kill anything," Lacey murmured. "She was a good shot and knew how to handle a weapon, but she wouldn't kill for sport."

Lacey looked away, her throat working.

"Um, how did you know Fawn?" Dr. Rhodes asked.

"We were very close," Lacey said. Which was completely true. She met the doctor's gaze and smiled.

"I see." He still looked confused as to the relationship, but Creed let it go.

"Thank you for your time. If you think of anything else, will you call?"

"Of course."

Creed stood and Lacey did the same. Only she staggered slightly. Creed snagged her upper arm and lowered her back into the chair. "Whoa. What's going on?" He knelt to look in her eyes, noting her suddenly pale face. A sheen of sweat had broken out across her forehead.

"Nothing," she said, waving him off. "Sorry. I just felt a little dizzy when I stood."

Dr. Rhodes rounded the desk and knelt in front of her. "Let me just check you out here."

Lacey held up a hand. "It's really not necessary. I think it's just that I haven't eaten much in the last few days."

"That could be it," the doc said, "but I'd

feel better if you'd let me have a listen and check your blood pressure and pulse. In spite of my fancy title as Research Director and pretty office, I really am licensed to practice medicine."

After a moment of hesitation, Lacey gave a short nod. "Fine. Thank you."

Dr. Rhodes checked her out, then stood and walked to the front of his desk. "Blood pressure is fine, heart sounds good. We can figure out if it's your blood sugar fairly easily." He opened a drawer and pulled out a pack of crackers. "Any allergies? Peanuts? Gluten?"

"No, nothing."

He handed her the crackers. "Eat these. If it's low blood sugar, those should help."

Instead of arguing, Lacey ate the crackers, and to Creed's relief, within a few minutes, color started to return to her cheeks. "You should go home and get some rest," Dr. Rhodes said. "And eat a good meal of mostly protein and healthy carbs."

Lacey nodded. "I'll do that. Thank you."

The doctor glanced at his watch. "I'm sorry. I'm late for another meeting."

"Of course," Creed said. "Sorry to keep you, but thank you for talking to us."

The doctor smiled, but it was tinged with real sadness and grief. "I hate the reason for it. I'm going to miss Fawn. We all will." His eyes misted and he shook his head. "But," he said to Lacey, "thank you for letting me use this." He tapped the stethoscope he'd placed back around his neck. "These days, it sometimes feels like it's all for show. Mere decoration so I look the part. Take care of yourself, and I really hope you find Fawn's killer soon."

"Thank you. I do, too." He left through his back door, and Lacey, Scarlett and Creed went out the main one to find the administrative assistant on the phone. She waved and they continued their trek to the elevator.

"Ready to get something to eat?"

"I think that's probably a good idea."

"Want to head across the street to the diner for a burger or a salad?"

"A burger sounds great."

Creed let Lacey lead the way, then got in front of her to hold the door for her and Scarlett.

His phone rang and he stopped to glance at the screen. "I need to take this."

"I'll get us a table."

He nodded and watched her step into the crosswalk, Scarlett at her side. The roar of an engine caught his attention. The sleek black Mustang in the lane raced down the street.

Straight toward Lacey and Scarlett.

NINE

"Lacey! Stop! Watch the car!"

Creed's frantic shout froze her. The engine of the approaching car reached her. She stopped. Then realized the vehicle had changed course, driving on the wrong side of the road, to aim right at her and Scarlett.

Lacey pulled on the leash. "Heel!"

She spun to run back toward the hospital sidewalk with Scarlett close at her side. Spectators screamed and ran, desperate to get out of the car's reckless path.

Lacey bolted behind a cement column, pulling Scarlett with her. Tires squealed, and when the Mustang hit the column, the impact sent vibrations through her body while pieces of cement rained down over her. But the column held.

"Lacey!" She heard Creed calling her name, sounding like he was far away. But then his hands were wrapped around her upper arms and his petrified gaze met hers. "Are you okay?"

"Yeah, yes, I'm fine." At least, she thought so. "Scarlett!"

The dog rose up on her hind legs and planted her paws on Lacey's chest. She hugged the dog, then gathered her wits. "Who is it?" she asked. "Who's in the car?"

But Creed was already moving toward it. Sirens sounded.

"There he goes!" The shout pulled her attention to the figure running from the scene. The spectator pointed. "Someone stop him!"

Creed put on a burst of speed and Lacey hurried to the car. The seat would have to do as an article for Scarlett. "Scarlett, scent." She pointed to the seat. "Get the scent, girl."

Scarlett went to work, pushing her nose at the leather. Then she backed up and Lacey let the lead out to let her go. Scarlett took off like a shot, heading in the same direction as Creed. Lacey dodged people and other vehicles, trying to keep up with the dog while making sure Creed stayed in her line of sight.

The man who'd nearly run her and Scarlett over disappeared around the side of a building and Creed ran after him. By the time Lacey caught up with him, he was breathing hard and looking frustrated.

"You lost him?"

"Yeah. He just vanished."

Scarlett had her nose in the air and darted to the back door of one of the businesses, then looked back at Lacey.

"She wants to go in."

Creed tried the handle. "It's locked."

"Well, he didn't float through the door."

"He didn't have time to pull out a key. My guess is it was propped open, and he went through it, then locked it behind him."

"Then he would have gone straight through and out, right?"

"Probably."

Lacey took off once more, this time leading Scarlett to the business's front door. "I'll check inside just in case," Lacey said.

"I'll hang out here and see if I spot him."

She nodded and led Scarlett inside, ignoring the looks of the patrons. "Anyone see a guy come running through here and out the door?"

"I did." A little girl about eight stuck her sucker back in her mouth.

"And he went out the door?" Lacey asked.

"Yep. He was running fast, too. Almost knocked me down." She scowled. "That was mean."

"It sure was." She paused. "Did he still have on a mask or could you see his face?"

"He had on a mask. It was kinda scary, but he was in a hurry."

Lacey rushed to the door and looked out. Creed stood on the sidewalk, hands on his hips, scowl on his face. He spotted her and shook his head.

"Can I pet your dog? What's his name?" The little girl had come up behind her and stood patiently waiting for Lacey's answer.

"This is Scarlett. She's working right now. Maybe when she's off duty. Okay?"

"Okay. I know all about special dogs like her."

"Tabitha? Tabitha? Where are you?"

"That's my mom."

"I figured."

"Lacey Lee?"

The voice came from behind her, and she turned to see her friend from high school with a newborn strapped to her chest and clutching the hand of a toddler. "Jessica?"

"Yes." The dark-eyed, dark-haired woman blinked at her. "You're back?"

"Yes. I came looking for Fawn because she wasn't answering her phone—and found her."

"I just heard about an hour ago. I'm so very sorry."

"Thank you." Lacey backed toward the door. "I'm kind of in a hurry, but call me and let's catch up sometime." Jessica nodded and Lacey looked at the little girl. "Thank you for your help."

"Anytime."

Lacey smiled at the grown-up response, then pushed through the door and out into the sunshine to find Creed waiting for her. They walked to his cruiser, keeping an eye on the traffic. When they stopped at the wreckage, Regina stepped forward. "Hey. You two okay?"

Creed hung up and nodded. "We're fine. The guy got away. He obviously wasn't hurt bad enough to slow him down any."

"Well, the car's stolen and the owner reported it about five minutes after it happened. He wasn't happy."

"He's not going to be any happier when he sees the condition."

"Yeah, I didn't mention that part."

"Okay," Creed said, "I'm going to let you, Ben and Mac finish up here while I take Lacey home. I'll get her statement and do mine as well, and I'll email it to you later tonight."

"We've got this."

"Thanks."

Lacey watched Creed work and realized that, in spite of the pain she blamed on him, she admired him greatly. He was a professional through and through and hadn't let their past hurts influence that professionalism. Whereas she'd arrived in town expecting someone to try and knock the chip off her shoulder.

The little spiritual tap on her conscience made her grimace. *Sorry, God. Forgive me, please.*

She waited for Creed to finish, and they walked together to his cruiser, where she buckled in Scarlett, then climbed into the passenger seat once more.

Creed aimed the vehicle toward Fawn's home—she was having trouble calling it *her* home—and Lacey rubbed a hand down her face. "All right. I need to think."

"Which means—"

"I talk."

"That's what I was going to say."

She wrinkled her nose at him. "Sorry. So..."

"So..."

"So, something happened, and Fawn decided she needed to take a three-month leave of absence from the hospital."

"But we don't know what happened."

"No, that's the key. When we know what caused her to do that, I have a feeling the trail will lead straight to her killer. But we don't know that yet. So, let's focus on what we do know."

"She went back to work for two days and then disappeared again. She had to have been killed after her shift on her second day back and before her next shift the third morning."

Lacey steeled herself against the grief and forced herself to view this as a case, not a loss. "But during the two days back at work, she looked tired, sad, worn down, troubled. Right?"

He nodded. "So, why go back to work if she was feeling bad?"

"Well...she wouldn't if she was contagious. But if she'd just had a bad night or something was bothering her emotionally..."

"She'd force herself to go because she'd already been gone for three months and didn't want to miss any more days?"

"Exactly. That would be like Fawn. She's always had a very strong work ethic—which is why her taking off for three months—and hiding it from me and everyone else—just doesn't make sense unless something was very, very wrong."

"Maybe she and the doctor broke up and she was trying to get past the worst of the hurt."

She shook her head. "Now, that I don't see." She pursed her lips. "But then, I wouldn't have seen a lot of this, so whatever it was, it was something she couldn't talk to me about." And that only added to her heart-shattering grief.

Creed pulled into Lacey's drive and shut the engine off. "You're coming in?" she asked.

"Do you mind? I want to check out your house."

She tilted her head and narrowed her eyes. "You don't think I'm capable?"

"More than, but I think we've discussed that it doesn't hurt to have backup occasionally. And after the attack at the gym and—"

"Almost being roadkill?"

"I would have put it a little differently than that, but yes."

She nodded. "Of course. You're right. I'd appreciate that."

They climbed out of the car, and he pointed to the open area across from the shed where they'd found Hank. "That'd be the perfect spot for a kennel."

She raised a brow at him. "So you've said."

"I know." He quirked a smile. "Just making sure you're paying attention." He let his gaze roam the land. "Lots of level land. What more do you need?"

"That's cute, Creed. You know as well as I do I'd need a lot more than just the land."

"But it'd be a start, right?"

Lacey backed toward the door, her gaze thoughtful.

"Let's go inside," he said. "We've been so busy dodging bullets and cars that we haven't had a chance to talk a little about your position with the department."

"My position?" She led the way into the house, and once again, the new-home smell hit him. Wood, stain and paint. Plus a hint of whatever shampoo Lacey used. She'd been back fewer than two days and already she'd left her mark on the place.

Scarlett found a spot in front of the fireplace and settled her nose between her paws. Before Creed took his seat on the couch, light snores from the dog reached him. "I guess she's tired."

"She's been busy lately." Lacey dropped into the wingback chair next to the bookcase and lowered her face into her hands.

"Lacey?"

She looked up. "Sorry, I'm just thinking."

"About?"

"That I need to be a big girl and admit I was wrong about the people in this town." She blew out a low breath. "I let fear keep me away. Fear of what I thought I remembered about this place. Fear of facing what my father had done. Fear of facing the people he'd done it *to*. Fear of—" she looked away from him "—a lot of things."

Fear of running into him—which she'd already mentioned. "And now?"

She met his gaze. "I like my life in Charlotte, Creed. It's a good life. If Fawn hadn't...wasn't...*dead*... I wouldn't be here and be so..."

"So what?"

"Confused!" The word burst from her, and she groaned, then dropped her head against the back of the chair. "I'm confused."

"Because?"

"Because I don't hate it here as much as I thought I would."

Creed's heart leaped in his chest and he immediately squashed the surge of hope. She might not hate it here, but she'd just told him how much she loved her life in Charlotte. "I'm glad," he said softly.

"Yeah, me, too. People have been really nice. That's probably due to Fawn staying and being her irresistible self. And now that she's dead, I guess no one wants to add to the pain by reminding me of the past. Maybe. I don't know." She shrugged and cleared her throat. "But that's not what you wanted to talk about." She clasped her hands and leaned forward. Then stood. "Oh. Before we talk about that position, I want to check Fawn's desk." She grabbed the keys from Fawn's gym bag.

"Good idea." He followed her into the guest room. All of the furniture had been put in storage while the floors were being done, but a small desk with a drawer and file cabinet stood in the center of the room, facing the window.

"Guess I'll have to look into getting her stuff out of storage."

"Well, it won't be hard to figure out where she had it. There's only one storage facility in Timber Creek."

"At least you have one."

She walked to the desk and tried the drawer. It slid open. "Well, it's not locked, but let's see if one of the keys works." The third one fit the desk. "Good to know. All right, she's got pens, pencils, a notepad, a bag of M&M's, stapler and paper clips. That's about it."

"I would think she'd keep all of her paper stuff in files."

"She would." Lacey tugged on the top drawer of the built-in two-drawer file cabinet. It slid open. "Okay, not locked either."

"Most people don't keep their file cabinets locked at home."

"I do."

"Well, you're in law enforcement."

She shot him a tight smile, pulled out a stack of hanging folders and passed them to him. She took a handful, and together, they made their way to the kitchen, where they went through each folder. She finally came to a piece of paper that stopped her. "It's a list of usernames and passwords. Oh, thank you, thank you, Fawn. We can get into her phone records and anything else we need."

"Perfect."

"Since I have no idea where Fawn's laptop is, I'm going to get mine. Be right back."

When she returned, he pulled the chair around beside her and they went through Fawn's cell phone records first. "Would you have any reason to know any of these numbers?" he asked her.

"No, but that's a hospital extension." She called it and Creed waited. "Oh, sorry. Wrong number." She hung up. "That was Dr. Charles Rhodes. Hopefully, he won't bother calling me back, thanks to the different area code on my number."

"She called him a lot and vice versa."

"Well, they were working on that project together."

"Yeah, but at ten o'clock at night?"

She frowned. "That is kind of suspicious." A sigh slipped from her. "You think he was the one she was involved with?"

"Hard to say, but not out of the realm of possibility."

"I just can't see her involved with a married man. That's so not Fawn."

"Several calls to this number." He rattled it off and she nodded.

"That's Miranda's number." She pointed. "And that's mine. And that's Jill Holloway's." She sighed. "What if I print this off and you have someone go through each number? This could take forever and I want to look at her credit card statements."

"Sounds good."

She set the printer in motion and moved on to the next website. "She only had two credit cards. One to the home improvement store, and the other looks like it was used for groceries and other odds and ends. Nothing weird on there and she paid it off when she got the bill. I hate to say it, but I don't think her phone records or credit cards are going to tell us anything."

"Print those out, too, for the last three months. I'll have Ben or Regina go through them when they have time."

"Sure."

When he had the printout tucked into his back pocket, she rested her chin on a fist and looked at him. "So, about that position..."

"I've been rethinking the offer."

She blinked. "Oh. Okay, then."

"Not as in I don't want you here. I do. But since you've made it obvious you're heading back to Charlotte, why don't we start interviewing people for the lead position? Help me find dogs without breaking the budget. You know, that kind of thing? Be my consultant."

"Sure, we can do that."

"Perfect. I'll put an ad in the online law enforcement journal and see if we get some bites." He paused. "Um, no pun intended."

This time her laugh was genuine, and it wrapped around him like a warm blanket. "I've missed that," he said. "I've missed *you*, Lacey." He missed her laughter, her goofy sense of humor, her listening ear. He missed kissing her. A lot.

She sighed and a sad longing flickered in her eyes. "I've missed you, too, Creed, but it makes no sense to revisit old feelings when it will just lead to heartbreak when it's time for me to leave again."

He studied her, turning her words over in his mind. "Yeah, you're probably right." He still wanted to kiss her, though. But more than that, he wanted to convince her to stay and give them another chance.

"Change of subject?" she asked.

"Okay."

"When do you think the ME will have the autopsy done?"

Her voice cracked, and it was all he could do not to get up and go to her, pull her into his arms—

"I don't know," he said, keeping himself firmly planted in his seat. "Shouldn't be too much longer. You heard Zeb. He has a backlog of cases, but I imagine we'll hear something tomorrow. If not, I'll call him."

Lacey nodded. "Not that there's a hurry, I guess, other than to have Fawn's funeral." Her jaw tightened and she looked away. "I can't believe I'm talking about burying my sister."

"Aw, Lacey, I wish I could do something to—"

"Catch her killer, Creed." Her shimmering eyes met his and the pain there took his breath away. "That's all I need."

He couldn't stand it. He stood, crossed the room and pulled her into his arms. She buried her face against his chest and let out a sigh that sounded like she'd finally come home. With one finger, he lifted her chin and searched her eyes, hoping she'd read the question in his. "Oh, Creed," she whispered. "I've missed you so much."

He couldn't do it. Kissing her right now when she was grieving and vulnerable would be taking advantage, and he considered himself way far above something like that. Instead, he pressed his lips to her forehead. "I know, Lacey, but we just agreed now isn't the time to revisit our old feelings."

"Is it wrong to want to?" she asked, her voice soft and barely there.

"No. I feel the same way, but you're leaving and I'm staying and that's that. Neither one of us believes in having a fling, so let's not open ourselves up for another world of hurt by thinking anything we might have now won't crash and burn with your exit."

She didn't answer but didn't protest either. Clearing his throat, he stepped back. He wouldn't survive losing her a second time, so it was better to let her go now. "Okay, so here's the plan. I'm going to fix you another meal full of protein and healthy carbs, and you're going to rest. Deal?"

"But—"

"Don't argue. Those crackers were good enough to tide you over for a while, but you need real food. Let me do this for you, okay?"

She nodded. "Okay."

TEN

Lacey's phone woke her early the next morning, the insistent alarm finally dragging her out of her heavy sleep. With a pounding head and a mouth full of cotton, Lacey struggled to remember why she felt so horrible.

Scarlett nudged her, then swiped a tongue over Lacey's cheek. "Thanks, girl. I know you need to go out. Hang on a sec." She rolled out of bed and into the bathroom while Scarlett waited with her usual patience.

In the middle of brushing her teeth, last night finally came back to Lacey in flashes. Creed had insisted she eat a protein-filled meal that he'd fixed for her with the contents of Fawn's fully stocked refrigerator. And then she'd taken a sleep aid and fallen into bed while he promised to keep watch on the house. After her three-month sabbatical—or whatever one wanted to call Fawn's absence—she'd grocery shopped and filled up her fridge and freezer like nothing was wrong. Like she'd never been gone.

Lacey rinsed her mouth and stared at her reflection. "Where were you for those three months, Fawn?" Because it wasn't here. Was it? Had Fawn been here for the whole three months, hiding away like a hermit while she dealt with whatever it was she needed to deal with?

And what about her mail?

Lacey finished up her morning routine, then made her way into the den, where she found Creed sitting up on the couch, his phone pressed to his ear. "Yeah. Got it. I'll ask her." He looked up and his gaze met hers. "Give me five minutes to get everything set up." He hung up.

"You need Scarlett?"

"And you." He rubbed a hand down his cheek. "Ben's outside keeping an eye on things so I could grab some sleep. He just let me know that his aunt called him. She works at the assisted-living home next door to the hospital and one of their residents was found missing this morning."

She let Scarlett out and nodded to Creed. "I'll get ready. Will you let Scarlett back in when you hear her bark?"

"Sure."

Within ten minutes, Lacey was ready and she, Creed and Scarlett were in Creed's cruiser and heading toward the facility. "I just thought of something this morning," she said. "Will you check with the post office and see if Fawn stopped her mail service for those three months?"

He cut her a sideways glance. "Good thought. Yeah, I can do that." He activated the Bluetooth and called Mac, asking him to look into Fawn's mail service.

"Got it. I'll text you what I find out in case you can't talk."

"Perfect."

When they arrived, a woman in her late forties was waiting for them at the entrance to the large brick-and-cream-siding building. Six white columns lined the front porch, with steps leading to the massive double oak doors. Creed parked. "That's Ben's aunt, Rianne Matthews."

"I think I remember her from church."

They climbed out. Lacey released Scarlett from her safety restraint and snapped the lead onto her harness.

Rianne rushed down the steps. She held a paper bag and thrust it toward Lacey. "Thank you so much for coming so fast. Our missing resident is named Ethan Mays. This is the shirt he wore yesterday. I figured you'd need it."

"Yes, ma'am," Lacey said. She took the bag. "Do you know which way he headed?"

"Not exactly. We have security cameras, of course, but we didn't see how he got out. However, I have my suspicions. In the basement, where they do the laundry, the workers sometimes leave the door open because it gets so hot in there from the dryers." She closed her eyes. When she opened them, tears shimmered. "The cameras show an orderly checking on him, and then five minutes later, Ethan walks out of his room and down the hallway to the exit. When he comes out at the bottom of the stairwell, he's on the first floor, but then he goes to the basement stairs and disappears. If the door at the bottom wasn't properly closed and locked, then I'd say that's how he managed to get out of the building."

Lacey nodded to the fence. "Can he get off the property?"

"I wouldn't think so. Not unless he managed to climb the fence. But it's a huge area. We have seventy acres, a lot of it wooded. And..." She gulped. "There's a large pond that some of the residents use for fishing and supervised swimming when the weather permits. It's on the other side of the back fence, but there's a gate and there are areas that need repairs. The repairs are on the schedule for this week, but since it's been so cold, and we haven't been using it..." She waved a hand. "Never mind all that. What's important is finding Ethan as quickly as possible."

She swiped a tear from her cheek and Lacey patted the woman's shoulder. "We'll do our best." Lacey opened the bag and held it out for Scarlett to get a whiff. "Scarlett, find Ethan. Find." Lacey tapped her pocket with the tennis ball.

Scarlett danced in a circle, her ears flying around her head, then shoved her nose at the bag once more. When she pulled back, she lifted her snout and sniffed one way, then another. She walked to the porch, then trotted around the side of the building and stopped. "I'd like to take her down to the exit," Lacey said, "where you think Ethan might have left. I think she'd have a better chance of getting the scent from there."

"Follow me."

The woman led the way and Scarlett trotted next to Lacey, through a maze of hallways, then down a set of stairs that led to the basement. Lacey let Scarlett have another sniff and the dog went straight to the exit. Lacey looked at Rianne. "Looks like your suspicions are right on target."

Rianne pushed the door open and Scarlett darted out with Lacey right behind. Lacey let the lead slacken and Scarlett raced toward the bench in the little garden about twenty yards away. The whole area was beautifully landscaped and the spring flowers were starting to bloom, but this early in the morning, there was a chill in the air that put the temperature in the low forties.

Creed kept pace with her. "This feels familiar."

"Hank?"

"Yeah."

She shot him a glance. "Let's pray the ending is just as happy."

"Exactly."

Scarlett loped toward the back of the property, where the wrought iron fence stretched long and far. She stopped and looked to her left, ears lifting, attention focused.

"What does that mean?" Creed asked.

"I don't know. Something distracted her."

"Scarlett, seek." Lacey waved the bag at the dog and Scarlett focused once more. She trotted to the fence, then started looking for a way through it. "He must have climbed over," Lacey said. She glanced the length of the fence within her sight range. "I don't see any area that needs repair here." Scarlett rose on her hind legs and placed her paws on the wrought iron. "She definitely wants to get to the other side."

"Then I guess that's what we'll have to do." He looked at her, then Scarlett. She knew exactly what he was thinking.

"It'll work," she said.

"What?"

"I'll go over first and you pick Scarlett up and over the fence and I'll help her down."

He blinked. "That's kind of scary that you can still read me so well, but yeah, that's exactly what I was thinking."

Just like the old days. She'd almost always known what he was thinking. *Almost.* She'd even known he had plans to be the sheriff of Timber Creek one day. She'd thought he would either wise up to his potential or she could change his mind and convince him he was better than a small-town sheriff. Her selfishness hit her square between the eyes and she almost lost her grip on the bars.

Stop it! Focus on finding Ethan.

Lacey cleared the wrought iron fence, grateful the top was a flat black piece and not spikes that could have been dangerous to navigate. She dropped to the ground and turned to find Creed lifting Scarlett over. She wrapped her arms around the solid animal and lowered her to the ground. Scarlett took off at a run and Lacey fell into step behind her, clutching the lead. Creed's footsteps pounded behind her and they slipped into the wooded area.

"There's a path," she said. "Scarlett's right on it. I feel sure Ethan came this way."

Scarlett led them through the woods, following the dirt path. "She's taking us to the pond," Creed said.

They broke through the tree line and into a small clearing. Lacey paused and Scarlett kept her nose in the air. "That's a pond?" Lacey asked. "Looks like a small lake to me. The water actually looks clean."

"Yeah, there's a little beach next to the dock. And two canoes."

"I'm sure the residents love it, but…"

"Yeah. This could be a problem if Ethan came this way."

Scarlett tugged at the lead and Lacey let her go. She led the way to the dock, and the bad feeling in Lacey's chest grew with each step.

She spotted something on the wood and walked out on the dock. "Hey, Creed? I found something. A rubber worm. I think he was here." She leaned over to pick up the item and something whipped over her head.

"Lacey!"

She turned at his running footsteps. He

dived at her, wrapped his arms around her and yanked her into the cold water.

It was April and it wasn't exactly warm above the water, but pond water in the spring was cold enough to steal his breath. The chill soaked through his skin into the depths of his bones. Creed kicked, aiming for the surface. He'd surprised Lacey with his dive and he worried she hadn't had time to suck in a breath.

He broke through and gasped while Lacey did the same, coughing and sputtering. "Wha—" She wheezed in more air and coughed again.

He shook the water from his eyes, and before she could lambaste him, he grabbed her hand and pulled her toward the shelter of the dock. When his feet touched the bottom, he led her to one of the thick red cedar posts. And registered Scarlett's frantic barking. Then a splash. "Scarlett, come!" He didn't know if the dog would obey his voice or not, but Lacey was still trying to breathe and he needed the dog with him, not a target for whoever had sent that bolt whipping over Lacey's head.

The dog swam toward him and he hooked a free arm around her to pull her to him. She rested on his forearm, trusting him to keep her afloat.

"C-Creed?" Lacey said. He still had his other arm wrapped around her waist. "Wh-what are you doing?" she asked. Her teeth were already chattering. From the shock of his move as much as the cold, no doubt.

"Someone shot at you."

Her eyes widened. "Again?"

"Again."

She frowned and swiped the water from her face. "I didn't hear a gunshot."

"It wasn't a rifle. It was a crossbow bolt. I think. Some kind of arrow, anyway. Stay here with Scarlett." He ignored her croaked protest and slogged his way to the edge of the dock. He peered around the last post. Nothing on the beach area caught his attention. But behind the trees...

He stepped out for a better look at the

movement, only to feel himself yanked backward the very moment he saw the flash of something headed toward him, then felt the sting of fire against his side. He yelped and slapped a hand over the burn. He spun to find Lacey narrow-eyed and furious. "Someone is shooting at us once more and you think you're invincible?"

Scarlett could touch bottom and was swinging her brown head back and forth between them, confused at the interruption of her search.

"No, I just—"

"Almost took a crossbow bolt through your gut." She moved toward him. "Let me see." Blood mingled with the water, but not so much that he was worried.

"I think it's just a graze, but thanks for pulling me back in time."

She shuddered and pushed his hand away, then peeled his shirt from the area. He hissed. "I need to call for backup."

"Is your phone working, by any chance?" she asked.

"Probably not."

She popped hers out of the clip on her belt and handed it to him. "The case is waterproof." At his raised brow, she shrugged. "I never know where Scarlett's going to take me. Or when I'm going to be dunked." She examined his wound and the touch of her cold fingers on his skin raised goose bumps all over. "It's more of a groove than a graze. You need stitches."

"Nah, it'll be all right."

He thought he heard her mutter "Stubborn" before she glanced at him. "Why don't you call whoever you need to while I keep watch on the woods?" She waded to the nearest post and peered around while he dialed 911 and waited for Dispatch to pick up.

"Nine-one-one. What's your emergency?"

"Nancy, this is Creed. I need backup out at the assisted-living pond. Someone's shooting a crossbow at us. Get everyone available out here. Who's the closest?"

"What?" Even as she asked the question, he could hear her fingers flying over the keys. "Are y'all okay? Um... Mac's on the way. In fact, he's less than a mile from your location. You should be hearing his siren soon."

"Good. Send Ben, too. And yes, we're fine." Discounting the fact that his side burned. But not as bad as he would have expected. The cold water was probably having a numbing effect.

"On it," the woman said. "I can get Regina out there, too, but she just took off on a personal errand, so it might be a while before she can get turned around."

"No, don't call her. By the time she could get here, I'm hoping we'll have this under control."

"Ten-four." More clicking. "Ben is on his way, as well."

"Thank you." He hung up and kept his gaze on the tree line.

Scarlett barked and headed toward the shore. Lacey grabbed her lead and pulled her up. "Scarlett, stay." The dog stopped, but her focus was on the wooded area just visible from their position under the dock.

"She hears someone," Lacey said. "Or smells someone."

"So, they're still out there."

"I'd say yes."

Creed itched to go after the shooter, but he'd be too exposed between the dock and the trees to risk it. "Come on, Mac," he muttered.

No sooner had the words escaped his lips than he picked up the sound of a siren. Scarlett barked again and Creed noticed the movement behind the trees just ahead. He spotted the fleeing figure and darted after it.

"Creed!"

Her cry was one of frustration with him, not a warning of trouble or a need for help. He ignored her and kept going. She and Scarlett followed, but as soon as he reached the tree line, a motorcycle roared away in the distance. He used Lacey's phone to call Mac.

The deputy answered halfway through the first ring. "McGee here."

"The shooter got away on a motorcycle."

He assumed it was the shooter. No one else would have had a bike waiting. "Put a BOLO out on it. It had some red trim. I didn't get a plate. Ben is coming this way. See if he spots it."

"Ten-four. You okay?"

"Yeah. Fine. Just want this person caught."

"I'm on it."

Lacey caught up with him. Shudders racked her every so often, reminding him that he was freezing. And they still had a man to find. "We need to get some dry clothes and warm up."

"I'm not leaving until we find Ethan. Movement will keep me warm enough."

"Liar."

"Okay, well, I might be cold and uncomfortable, but I won't freeze to death. I'm heading back to the dock to get the rubber fishing worm I saw before you tackled me. And the bag for Scarlett. I dropped it when you shoved me into the water."

He nodded. "All right. I'm right behind you. Mac and Ben are chasing down the shooter." He pressed a hand to his throbbing side and found it had started bleeding once more. If it had ever stopped.

"We need to get you to the hospital," Lacey said, frowning at him. "You definitely need stitches."

He grimaced. The last place he wanted to go was the hospital. "After we find Ethan and only if Katherine is available to meet me there."

"Agreed."

Once Lacey retrieved the bag with Ethan's scent and Scarlett had gotten another good whiff, the dog raced toward the trees with Lacey right behind her.

ELEVEN

Lacey followed Scarlett, dodging limbs and the undergrowth. Scarlett continued to plow down the path. When she rounded the next tree, she slowed, her head moving, nose twitching. Straight ahead, Lacey spotted a bare foot at the same time Scarlett beelined for it.

"We found him, Creed. Call it in, will you?" He had the only working phone.

Lacey raced to the foot and touched it. Cold. But not deathly cold. She moved to Ethan's head and placed her fingers against his neck. "He's got a pulse!" He groaned and opened his eyes. When they landed on Lacey, he gasped and struggled to sit up. She helped him lean against the tree trunk. "Hi, Ethan. Don't be afraid. I'm here to help."

For a moment, when his eyes met hers, they sharpened. "What happened?"

"You wandered away from home, Mr. Mays—Ethan. Scarlett and I came to take you back."

He shivered and crossed his arms, his arthritic hands clasping his biceps. "Cold."

"I know. The paramedics are coming, and they'll have a nice warm blanket for you."

He frowned. "You're the one who needs the blanket. You're all wet."

She let out a laugh but couldn't help the tremor that shook her. "I f-fell in the pond."

"I wanted to go fishing."

"I saw the worm on the dock." The rubber worm that had saved her life. "Did you drop it?"

He rubbed his head. "I don't know."

"It's okay." She patted his hand. "Why don't we get you warmed up?"

He drew back. "No. I have to wait here."

"Why?"

"In case he comes back. He said he would get me a fishing rod."

Lacey caught Creed's eye, then looked back at Ethan. "Who said that?"

"The man."

"Did you know him?"

"I... I'm not sure. Seems like I might have known him, but I can't think of—" He slapped his head. "Ah! I can't remember!"

Lacey grabbed his hands before he could hit himself again. "It's okay, Ethan. Really, it's okay."

His eyes had clouded once more. "Who are you?"

"My name's Lacey."

Scarlett moved in front of Ethan and placed a paw on his knee. The man lifted a hand to run it over the dog's soggy head. "Nice dog."

"She is. Her name is Scarlett."

He rose to his feet. "I had a dog."

"Hold on. The paramedics are coming to make sure you're all right and then take you to the hospital."

"No. I don't want doctors." He pulled away from her and stumbled. Creed caught him and held him while Ethan muttered, "No doctors. Don't like doctors." While he spoke, his hands sought out Scarlett's soggy ears. He rubbed and the dog moved closer, her eyes intent, seeming to understand the man's fragile state.

"Ethan," Creed said, "it's all right. Scarlett will stay with you."

Ethan looked down. "Good dog."

He started to walk, his hand on Scarlett's back, and Creed moved to stop him. Lacey snagged Creed's fingers. "Let him walk. He doesn't appear to have any serious injuries. He's awake, he's talking and he's going in the right direction. Scarlett's helping him keep his balance. The faster we go, the faster he gets any help he might need."

Creed stayed close to the man's side, ready to catch him should he need to. He looked back at her. "I want to know who told him he'd take him fishing."

She nodded. "Once we get him turned over to the paramedics, you need to go back and collect that worm. It's evidence.

Someone gave it to him and enticed him down to the dock."

"Yeah." He nodded, his face thoughtful, tense. "And... I think whoever that person was knew I'd ask you and Scarlett to come hunt for him."

Lacey let her brain wrap around the thoughts coming at her. "Well, after the story in the paper about our role in Hank's rescue and Fawn's death, it wouldn't take a rocket scientist to figure out if an elderly Alzheimer patient went missing..."

"I'd call you," Creed finished. "Yeah."

"This was a setup, wasn't it?"

"I can't say for sure, obviously, but... I'm leaning toward that conclusion. Especially since we were sitting ducks out here near the pond." He shivered and narrowed his eyes. "I'm freezing. Come on. I want to see security footage at the facility and find out everyone Ethan came into contact with."

"A shower and some dry clothes would be nice, too."

"And that."

Lacey heard the paramedics before she saw them. They stepped out of the tree line, and she recognized the two paramedics hurrying toward them. Annie Kitts and Hannah Ligon. "Hi, Lacey," Annie said. "Glad to have you back."

Hannah stared at Lacey, her eyes guarded and cold. Hannah's parents had been victims of her father's crimes. Annie's had not.

"Hi," Lacey said. "This is Ethan Mays. He's cold, but doesn't appear to be hurt. We found him asleep, but not unconscious."

Annie and Hannah went to work. Lacey stepped up to Ethan and placed a hand on his shoulder. "I'm glad you're okay."

His eyes met hers, clear again for the moment. "Thank you." He patted Scarlett's head.

"Ethan?"

"Yes?"

"Who gave you the worm?"

"The man. Said to come to the dock to go fishing."

"What was his name?" She had to try, now that he seemed to be "back."

"I don't know. He looked familiar, but I don't know why." Ethan closed his eyes. When he opened them, desperation flashed at her. "I have trouble with my memory a lot. I'm sorry."

"It's okay."

Hannah sighed. "Can you move? We have a job to do, you know."

Lacey frowned at the woman's rudeness, but decided not to address it. "Yeah, sure."

She stepped back and met Annie's gaze. "Could you check Creed's side? He got grazed by a crossbow bolt."

"What?"

"Lacey, I'm fine."

Creed and Annie spoke at the same time.

Lacey crossed her arms and stared at him until he sighed. "Fine." He pulled up his torn shirt and Annie leaned in for a look.

"Ouch," Lacey said. "That looks even more painful than my first glimpse in the water."

"A bit."

"It's still bleeding, too," Lacey pointed out.

Creed narrowed his eyes at her. "It'll stop."

"You need stitches," Annie said, "and possibly an antibiotic. No telling what's in that water. You should probably head to the hospital."

Lacey nodded. "Okay, we'll go there now."

"Hold on a second—"

"What if it was me, Creed? What would you make me do?" He sighed and muttered something she missed. "I'm sorry—could you repeat that?"

"I said fine, I'll go to the hospital and get checked out."

"That's what I thought you said."

"Let's go."

Hannah's gaze hadn't left Lacey. "You shouldn't have come back here," the woman blurted. "We're all still trying to forget the devastation your father left behind. You showing up just brings back a bunch of bad memories."

"Hey now, Hannah. That's not nec—" Creed started to protest.

"Well, if someone hadn't killed my sister," Lacey interrupted, "I wouldn't be here. But don't worry. As soon as her killer is found, I'm out of here."

Hannah flinched. "Yeah. Sorry about Fawn," she muttered.

"I am, too." Lacey walked away and Creed fell into step beside her, his hand searching for hers. He squeezed and Lacey drew in a shaky breath even as she took comfort in his touch. "I don't know why I still let people get to me. I thought I had developed a thicker skin."

"Hurtful words still hurt."

True enough. "I guess Fawn didn't remind her of our father and his crimes, but I do. Wow." Lacey did her best to shrug off the pain and focused on the fact that she really liked holding Creed's hand.

Which was why she pulled away.

She was leaving. Falling in love with

Creed again would only cause her—and him—more damage than what a few barbed comments did. The kind of pain that there were no words for. She'd been there and done that and wasn't interested in a repeat performance. They'd settled this last night, so why was she revisiting it?

"Here," Annie said, walking up to them. She held two blankets. "Use these and get them back to me at some point, will you?"

"Thanks." Lacey ignored Creed's narrow-eyed scrutiny and took one of the blankets. Creed did the same, and side by side, with Scarlett's lead clutched in her right hand, they walked to his cruiser. "I think I should probably drive. I'm not the one that's been bleeding everywhere."

"I can't let you drive. Official vehicle rules and all that."

"I would think you could make an exception here?"

"Nope."

"And if you pass out at the wheel?"

He slid her a glance that held a mixture of amusement and pain. "I promise

I wouldn't drive if I thought I was going to pass out." He paused. "If at any point I start feeling woozy, I'll pull over and call for Regina or Ben to come get us."

She sighed. "Fine, but I'm going to be watching you very closely."

"I wouldn't expect anything different."

Once they were all buckled in, he cranked the engine, flipped the heat on high, then pulled into the street.

"Hospital," Lacey said.

"Yeah, yeah. But I'm calling Katherine to ask her to meet me there—assuming she's not already there."

"Works for me."

He activated the Bluetooth and managed to track down their doctor friend, who promised to meet them at the emergency room.

Now, if they could just get there without anything else happening, Lacey might be able to catch her breath.

Creed pulled into the police-reserved hospital parking spot and shut off the engine. Lacey had been true to her word and watched him like a hawk all the way. He really would have made other arrangements had he felt woozy or like he was struggling to drive, but he still felt energized from the adrenaline rush. He figured he had another few minutes before it would crash and leave him shaking.

"Creed? You okay?" Lacey asked from the open passenger door. Scarlett was already out of the vehicle and waiting patiently at her side. He nodded and she shut the door.

Creed climbed out, stifling a gasp at the pain the movement caused. Lacey wrapped a hand around his biceps as though to hold him up. "If I fall, just get out of the way, okay? I'd squash you like a bug."

She laughed and the sound washed over him like a wave of warmth. His heart clenched, and once again, the pain of losing her flashed through his mind in vivid detail and saturated with heartache.

"Good to be compared to a bug."

"What? No, I'd never—"

"I'm teasing. Let's find Katherine."

Yeah, they needed to do that before he made a complete fool of himself. "I'm going to call my mother and ask her to bring us some dry clothes."

"That would be lovely."

"What size do you wear?"

She told him. "A brush would be nice, too. My hair needs some TLC in a very desperate way."

He paused. "May I use your phone?"

"Of course."

He took it and passed the information on to his mother, who demanded to know if he was all right. "Yes, I promise, I'm fine. And so is Lacey."

"Creed, be honest. I know you think you're protecting me by not giving me all the details, but I'll tell you right now, that just makes things worse."

"Mom—"

"Because my imagination can come up with all kinds of scenarios, as you know."

Boy, did he.

"Do I need to come stay with you? Take care of you? Bring you some food?"

"Just the clothes, please."

"Fine, but if I think you're hurt worse than you're letting on, I'm not going to be happy and neither will your father."

"I know. Thank you."

"I'll be on my way shortly. Give Lacey a hug for me."

"Will do. Thank you."

"I love you, Creed."

"I love you, too, Mom." He hung up and let out a slow breath, then a short laugh. His mother could be a force to be reckoned with and he loved her dearly.

"She doesn't hate me, does she?" Lacey asked.

"Hate you?" Creed eyed her. "Not at all. She told me to give you a hug. She's missed you."

"I've missed her, too. There were days she was more of a mother to me than my own mom."

He gave her a side hug and kissed the edge of her temple. "I know."

Lacey went still and Creed mentally slapped himself for initiating the intimate moment, then dropped his arm. "That was from Mom."

"Of course."

Katherine stepped into the waiting room, dissipating the awkward moment. She raised a brow. "What happened to you two? You look like drowned rats." Katherine's youthful features kept one guessing her true age. The only reason Creed knew how old she was and how well qualified she was in her profession was that he'd known her since they were kids.

"Long story," Creed said.

"Well, follow me. You can tell me while I'm doctoring whatever it is I'm doctoring."

Lacey nodded at him. "Scarlett and I'll just wait here."

"Oh no you don't," Creed said. "If I have to be checked out, so do you." He wasn't letting her out of his sight. Someone had just tried to kill her. Leaving her alone in the waiting room wasn't an option.

"What?" She gave a huff of laughter. "I'm not the one who got shot."

"Shot?" Katherine's eyes went wide and bounced between him and Lacey. "No one mentioned anything about bullets."

"It wasn't a bullet." Creed scowled. "It was a bolt from a crossbow."

"Oh well, then. Of course that's *so* much better." Katherine rolled her eyes and Creed noticed Lacey struggling to keep a straight face.

He lifted his jaw and narrowed his eyes at Lacey. "I'm not going unless you go, too."

"How old are you? Ten?" He kept his gaze steady, and Lacey threw up her hands in surrender. "Fine. I'm coming, too. Come on, Scarlett. Let's keep the baby company."

Creed snorted, Katherine laughed, and they all made their way through the double doors of the ER.

Katherine stopped in front of a room. "Um. Do you need separate rooms? Because it's kind of busy here and I'm not sure we have another one to spare."

"I don't need a room at all," Lacey said with a pointed look at Creed.

He grabbed her hand. "She can share mine." He pulled her through the door and pointed to a chair in the corner. "You take that." He looked at Katherine. "I imagine I need to lie down for this?"

"Probably best."

A nurse bustled into the room pushing an IV pole. "Which arm you want this in?"

"I don't need that."

"It's fluids and antibiotics," Katherine said. "You need it. It won't take long to go through the bag. Now, let me help you get your shirt off and this gown on."

Creed groaned, but let her have her way. Soon, he was stretched out on the gurney even while he shot a scowl at the nurse. "You get one try."

"Grumpy today, are we?"

"Sorry," Creed muttered.

"But—" she flashed him a tight smile that said he didn't intimidate her in the least "—the good thing is, I only need one stick. Trust me."

Lacey sat in the chair, a bemused expression on her face while the nurse aimed the needle at the inside of his left elbow. He flinched, but sat still until the woman looked up. "Good job," she said.

He blew out a breath. "I hate needles."

"Do you mind if I take a look now?" Katherine asked.

"Go for it."

She did, then leaned over and sucked in a breath. "Whoa."

"Whoa? Did you learn that diagnosis in med school?"

She gave his shoulder a light punch. "Cute." She stepped back and turned to Lacey, who pulled the blanket tighter around her shoulders. "Did you get shot, too?"

"No. Thanks to Creed, I'm fine. Just cold and wet and in need of a hot shower and dry clothes."

"All righty, then," Katherine said to Creed, "I'm going to get this cleaned up, numbed up and stitched up."

"That's a lot of *ups*," Creed said. "Like

two too many. You really think numbing and stitching are necessary?"

She met his gaze. "Absolutely. That bolt dug a nice groove in your side."

He sighed. "Fine."

"Told you so," Lacey said with a slight smirk.

He gave her a rueful smile and grimaced.

Katherine patted his hand. "You want anything for pain?"

"Nothing that will knock me out."

"All right. I've got something that'll take the edge off. It might make you a tad sleepy, but it definitely won't knock you out. Be back in a few." She whipped out the door and silence fell.

Creed shifted and winced. Lacey moved to sit on the bed beside him. "Thank you for saving my life," she said. "I have no doubt that bolt would have wound up hitting me if you hadn't acted."

He covered her cold hand with his and squeezed. "I'm just glad I saw it coming." He hadn't known what it was heading their way, just that the flash of whatever he'd seen probably wasn't good, and he'd reacted. "I hope Regina or someone managed to retrieve the bolts. We might be able to trace them back to where they were purchased from."

"And the worm."

"Maybe. It's possible they all came from the same place."

"I'm just mad that this person is dragging innocent people into whatever he's doing. Ethan Mays could have been seriously hurt—or worse."

"I know." He ignored the throbbing in his side and focused on one important fact. "I need a new phone."

"Can Ben or Regina grab one for you?"

"Yeah. Do you mind if I use yours to call and ask?"

She handed him the device for the third time and he worked out the details. He'd just hung up when the door opened once more and Katherine entered, holding a syringe in her right hand. "All righty, got something here that will have you feeling better in a few minutes. No new allergies, right?"

"Nope."

She dispensed the medicine into the IV port, then went to work cleaning the wound. When she sat back, she grabbed a suture kit. "All of the nurses are with other patients, so I'll just take care of this myself."

"I can't believe I'm letting you stick needles in me."

"Ha. That's funny. I used to beg you to be my patient and now I finally get to doctor you." Katherine had had a volatile childhood and had wound up living with Creed and his family for a while during her teen years. She was the sister he'd never had.

Fifteen minutes later, she was finished and he sported twelve new stitches and a white bandage. "Keep it clean and you'll be fine. I can take the stitches out in a couple of weeks."

"Thanks." He caught her hand. "I appreciate you taking the time to meet me here."

"I had patients to check on anyway, but even if I didn't, you know I don't mind. In fact, I would have been mad if you *hadn't* called."

"That's why I did."

"I'll look in on you in a bit." She looked at Lacey. Her phone buzzed and she glanced at it. "Creed's mom is here. I'm going to let her come see for herself that Creed and you are alive and kicking, but I'm going to encourage her not to stay long."

"Thank you," Lacey said. "Getting dry would be awesome."

She opened the door, and Creed's mother walked in, set a large bag on the floor and went straight for Creed. She stopped short of grabbing him but looked into his eyes. "You're all right?"

"Yes, Mom, I promise."

She turned her attention to Lacey. "And you're okay?"

"Yes, ma'am."

"Okay, then. I've been instructed not to linger, so I just need hugs and then I'm out of here until you tell me what else I can do to help. Your father sends his love. He stayed at the store, but said he'd close it and come if you needed him." His dad had owned the Timber Creek General Store since before Creed was born and took pride in serving the residents of Timber Creek. His mom gave him the once-over yet again. "He'll be relieved to know you're okay. I'll call him as soon as I get back in the car. Now, hugs, please."

Creed obliged. Then she went to Lacey and pulled her tight. "I've missed you, Lacey Lee."

"I've missed you, too, Mama Payne."

Creed's heart swelled along with the lump in his throat. It was good to see them together again.

"I can't tell you how sorry I am about Fawn," his mother said, her voice low, but he caught the words.

"Thank you."

"Come see me when you can."

"Yes, ma'am. I will."

Creed smiled as the door closed behind

her and he looked at Lacey. "Told you she didn't hate you."

"Yeah," she whispered.

Creed's lids grew heavy. The pain meds were working—and while he didn't feel like he *had* to sleep, they were relaxing him enough that the idea was appealing. He yawned. Lacey scooted forward and passed him some clothes. "I'm going to find another bathroom while you change. I'll also let someone know you need some new sheets. Then I'll be back."

He frowned. "Be careful."

"I will. I'm not going far. Then you can sleep for a while. You have until the IV bag empties. You might as well recharge."

It sounded like a pretty good idea to him. "Is there a guard on the door?"

Lacey nodded and snagged the bag with the rest of the things his mother had brought, then clicked to Scarlett. "Jimmy from Security is here. He's going to stay until we walk out of here."

Or trouble walked in.

TWELVE

She'd never take dry clothes for granted again. *Grateful* didn't come close to expressing her appreciation of the effort.

While Scarlett waited patiently next to the door, Lacey had managed a sponge bath in the bathroom, then washed her hair in the sink and toweled it dry before pulling it up into her usual ponytail. Then she cleaned the pond water and muck from Scarlett, much to the dog's mortification, but Lacey insisted and Scarlett had endured. "Well, you smell better," Lacey had muttered. "We'll do a better job later."

Scarlett had ignored her, still obviously miffed.

Once Lacey was dressed and clean, she'd emptied her weapon and dried it as best she could. She reloaded it and replaced it in the shoulder holster and decided she felt halfway normal. Even though her mind wouldn't shut off.

While Creed slept, Lacey scratched Scarlett's ears and mulled over a thought that had been niggling at the back of her mind ever since they'd walked into the hospital. Dr. Rhodes was a hunter. He'd been friends with Fawn. What if they'd been more than friends? What if he was the doctor she'd been seeing?

The very thought of her sister sneaking around with a married man made her stomach turn. It wasn't something she could even envision Fawn doing, but... she couldn't quite dismiss the possibility without a little investigation.

And then there was the crossbow. A hunter's weapon.

She needed to talk to Dr. Rhodes.

Creed looked like he might sleep for a while longer, so she rose and slipped out the door to walk to the nurses' station. "Could I have a pen and paper?"

The nearest nurse handed her the items, and Lacey returned to Creed's room, where she wrote him a short note about what she was going to do. He probably wouldn't be happy if he woke up and found her gone, but she wasn't going far and she'd be safe enough in a busy hospital.

And she'd have Scarlett with her, as well. Scarlett was a mild-mannered animal most of the time, but she was very protective of Lacey should the need arise.

Lacey left the note on the magnetic board that faced Creed's bed. As soon as he opened his eyes, he'd see it.

She gathered Scarlett's lead and left the room once more to make her way to the elevator that would take her to Dr. Rhodes's office.

When she arrived, she found the administrative assistant's desk empty, so she walked through to the doctor's office. The door was cracked. She knocked. "Dr. Rhodes?"

No answer.

Lacey gave the door a slight push and

it swung inward to reveal the inner office empty, as well. "Okay," she muttered. "What do you think, Scarlett? Should we see if we can find out the answer to one of the questions burning in my mind?"

Scarlett looked up and tilted her head as though trying to figure out what Lacey was saying. "Come on, girl." With Scarlett beside her, Lacey slipped into the doctor's office, shut the door behind her and walked to the credenza behind his desk to get a closer look at the display of pictures.

She already knew the man was a hunter, but most hunters used more than one weapon. She stepped closer, examining them one by one. And there it was.

A crossbow.

Rhodes stood with several other men she didn't know, but Tucker Glenn was there with his arm around Rhodes. Next to Tucker was Keith Webb, another high school friend who'd gone into law. He, Tucker and another partner had opened the only law firm in Timber Creek. Each man held a crossbow. That was what had been niggling at the back of her mind. She'd noticed the picture from her and Creed's visit.

Then again, there were probably quite a few people in Timber Creek who hunted with crossbows. Just because the doctor did didn't mean he was the one trying to kill her.

But someone was and this seemed the right place to start asking questions. She turned and her eyes fell on the doctor's desk. A pen like the one found on Fawn's property lay on top of a closed manila folder. Two more were in a mug next to his laptop. Not that the pens meant anything. Everyone in the hospital probably carried them.

She turned and caught her breath. She knew that shirt hanging on the hook. Fawn had bought it on her last visit with Lacey. They'd spent the weekend laughing and shopping, and Fawn had fallen in love with the top.

A door shut in the outer office and Lacey jumped. She really didn't want anyone to know she was here, so she headed for the other exit next to the credenza.

"I'm telling you," a man's voice said just outside the closed door. "I can't find it."

"And I'm telling *you*. We don't have a choice. You need to keep looking or we're all going to be in trouble." Dr. Rhodes sounded mighty upset about something.

Lacey ushered Scarlett out the door and quickly followed. She pulled the door almost shut behind her, leaving a thin crack to look through. Dr. Rhodes stepped into his office and looked back over his shoulder. "I don't have time to discuss this." He took his white lab coat from the hook behind the door and shrugged into it. "Just find the book and everything will be fine."

"I've got to go before I'm missed. I'll keep looking on my end. You keep looking on yours."

"Of course."

The other man's footsteps faded, and Lacey regretted she hadn't gotten a look at him. Security footage should help her figure out who he was. The conversation between the two men had been curious, but nothing incriminating. She didn't care about a lost book. She wanted to know who'd thought it'd be a good idea to lure a sick man out to the dock and then shoot to kill when she and Creed arrived.

She shut the door, careful to hold the handle so it made as little sound as possible, then turned to lead Scarlett down the three steps and into the hallway of the hospital.

Her phone buzzed and she didn't recognize the number. "Hello?"

"Where are you? Are you okay?"

"I'm fine, Creed." He must have used the landline next to his bed to call her. "I'm on the way back to your room right now."

"When I woke up and you weren't here—"

"Didn't you get my note?"

"Yeah, but anyone could have forced you to write that."

Ouch. He wasn't wrong. "I'm fine. Sorry I scared you."

"I'm ready to get out of here. As soon as you get here, we can leave."

"Ten-four." She picked up the pace and made her way back to his room in record time. She knocked.

The door opened and Creed stepped out, fully dressed in a clean long-sleeved T-shirt and jeans. Lacey's heart hammered. He'd changed a lot in the six years she'd been gone. From boy-man to full-grown man. She'd loved the boy-man, but now she almost couldn't pull her gaze from him. It wasn't even his looks, although he was certainly easy on the eyes, but it was more his attitude, his heart for the hurting, his desire to help the underdog. And when he looked at her the way he was doing now—

She cleared her throat. "Ready?"

"Yeah." He pressed a hand to his side.

"How are you feeling?"

"Not bad, but Ben and Regina are coming to pick up my cruiser and take you home. Katherine told me I couldn't drive, thanks to the drugs she fed me." He scowled. "I didn't think about that when I consented to take them."

"Most of the bedroom furniture is in storage, but you can come back to Fawn's house and crash on the couch for a while. I can fix you dinner and we can talk. I have some things I need to fill you in on." Like her impromptu office visit. "I'll take you home when you're ready."

He hesitated, then nodded. "Sounds good."

Ten minutes later, they were in a department-issued cruiser with Regina at the wheel, Creed in the front seat, and Lacey and Scarlett in the back. Creed programmed his new phone as he rode, and Lacey watched the mirrors, half expecting someone to ram them, shoot at them or even try to blow them up. She wanted to tell him about the picture and the pens in the doctor's office, but he was preoccupied at the moment and she didn't want to be distracted from watching their tail. However, she could tell he was still alert and aware of their surroundings since he looked up every few seconds.

They arrived at Fawn's house without incident and Regina pulled into the drive and cut the engine. "I'll just wait here until y'all give me the all clear to head out."

Lacey studied Fawn's front door. "I don't think that's going to happen anytime soon. Someone's either in Fawn's house right now, or they've been here and gone. Because I didn't leave that door cracked."

Creed pulled his weapon. "I'll go in first."

"Scarlett, stay." The dog settled back onto the seat. Lacey snagged her gun from her shoulder holster and aimed it at the door. "I'm right behind you."

"I'll go around the back," Regina said. She hurried off and Creed used his elbow to nudge the door open.

He stepped inside and sucked in a breath. "Uh-oh."

"What do you mean, uh-oh?" Lacey entered and moved to the side. "Well, that's just great."

"Yeah." Someone had trashed the place. Furniture upended, cushions slashed, lamps broken on the floor and bookshelves tossed.

She nodded to the hallway. "Let's clear the place. Then I'll have a look around."

Together, they walked through the house and returned to the living area. Creed holstered his weapon and notified Regina the house was clear. Lacey retrieved Scarlett from the vehicle. The dog stepped inside, her nose twitching. "Wish I could use her to find whoever did this," Lacey said.

"That would be ideal."

Scarlett hesitated, obviously confused by the chaos. Lacey pulled her bed out from under a couch cushion, cleaned the area in front of the fireplace and laid the bed in the spot. "Come here, girl. Scarlett, bed."

Scarlett bolted to her bed and settled on it, her eyes bouncing between Lacey and Creed.

Creed touched Lacey's arm. "I'll help you clean this up."

"You don't need to be cleaning. You need to be resting." She sighed and rubbed her eyes. "Why don't you let Regina take you home and I'll take care of this mess?"

"No way. I'm not leaving you here alone."

"Okay, fine." She went to the recliner and righted it. "At least they spared the upholstery on this. Make yourself comfortable here and I'll see if I can put the couch back together."

"The cushions are slashed."

"I'm aware, thanks." She picked one up. "But only on one side. I can sew the fabric back together and simply put the repaired side down."

"You can do that? Sew, I mean?"

She planted her hands on her hips and lifted her chin. "I'm not completely helpless in the domestic arena, you know."

He chuckled, then winced and pressed his side. He had to stop doing that for a while. "I didn't mean to imply that you were."

She pointed to the recliner. "Sit. Relax. Close your eyes. I'll go through the house and bag anything that might be considered evidence."

He lowered himself into the chair just as Regina stepped inside. Her eyes widened at the scene. "Wow. Someone's not happy with you, are they?"

Lacey grimaced. "Apparently not."

"I've gone around the property and found nothing to indicate anyone was here other than in the house." She glanced around. "I'll get the evidence collection kit from my cruiser."

"Thanks," Lacey said. Within seconds, she was back, and the pain in his side was such that Creed seriously wondered if he could rise from the chair should he need to.

"I've got this, Creed," Regina told him. "Lacey and I can work the scene. Stay put."

He hesitated, but with the eyes of both women lasering holes in him, he decided to cave. "All right."

"Good choice," Lacey muttered.

Creed's eyes may have closed. And he may have even slept, because the next thing he knew, he could hear Lacey walking back into the den. Funny how he knew it was her simply by the way she walked. What wasn't so funny was how very aware he was of her approach. She stopped next to him and he opened his eyes. The den was clean and the sofa looked like nothing had happened. She'd already sewn the fabric?

"How long was I out?" he asked.

"About three hours. Regina just left, but Ben said he was going to come by and keep an eye on the place. I'm going to work in the kitchen. While I'm there, I'll see if I can throw together a salad or something. I think there's a rotisserie chicken in there, too."

"Sounds good. I'll help."

"You will not," she snapped.

Her glare nearly singed him. "What? Why are you looking at me like that?"

"Because you're stubborn."

"Yes. I know."

"Rest, Creed, please? You need to heal."

A knock on the door startled both of them and Creed's hand went to his gun. She raised a brow at him. "I doubt the intruder is going to come back and knock."

"You never know," he muttered.

Lacey went to the window and glanced out. When she smiled, Creed's heart rate went down and he allowed his shoulders to relax a fraction.

Katherine stepped inside and shut the door behind her. "I came to check on my patient and make sure he's taking care of himself."

"He's obnoxious," Lacey said. "He wants to help me in the kitchen."

"That's a no, Creed." She gave him the same look Lacey had drilled him with. Did women practice that look? Whatever the case, it was very effective.

"Tattletale," Creed called out. He could easily see and hear them from his spot in the recliner.

She rolled her eyes at him and Katherine laughed. "Glad to see you two getting along so well." She held up three bags. "I brought dinner." In her other hand, she balanced three drinks.

Lacey's nose twitched, much like Scarlett's when she got the scent. "Oh yum, what?"

"Burgers, fries and shakes. Creed gets the peanut butter one. Lacey and I get the chocolate ones."

His stomach rumbled and he held out a hand. "You are the best sister a guy could ask for."

Katherine passed him the shake. Then she and Lacey each took an end on the couch and used the coffee table to hold the food. No one spoke for several minutes while they inhaled the burgers. Then Katherine took a sip of her shake and looked up. "How's the side?"

"Fine."

"Right." She pulled a small bag from her purse. "I brought some bandages in case you didn't have any. There's some antibiotic cream in there, too."

"Thanks."

"Where's Dominic?" Creed asked her.

"Debating whether or not to come home and help you find Fawn's killer."

Dominic O'Ryan was Katherine's husband of four months. He was also a US marshal and friend to Creed. "Who's he after now?"

"No one. He's guarding a judge who's been receiving death threats." She wiped her hands on a napkin. "He said to tell you he knows it's out of his jurisdiction, but he has some leave and he's willing to use it if you need some help guarding Lacey here." She eyed him. "Or if you need some guarding."

"That's generous of him, but I'm not ready to call in reinforcements just yet."

She nodded. "I'll tell him."

"And I need to tell you something that I discussed with Regina while you were sleeping," Lacey said.

"What's that?"

"I think Dr. Rhodes was the doctor Fawn was involved with."

THIRTEEN

Both Creed and Katherine looked at her like she'd grown another head, but the thought had been swirling around in her mind ever since she'd overheard Rhodes and the other man talking.

"You know Dr. Rhodes is highly respected at the hospital," Katherine said. "He's a family man and an all-around good guy. I don't see it."

"No one saw my father for what he was either," Lacey said, her tone sharper than she'd meant it to be.

Katherine grimaced. "Okay, I'll have to give you that one."

"I'm sorry. I'm not trying to be snippy. Just let me explain." She recounted her experience in Dr. Rhodes's office, explaining about Fawn's shirt being on the back of the door, then repeating the dialogue she'd heard. "And he's got a picture of him and some of the other men in town that he's friends with. They're all holding cross-bows."

Creed frowned. "A lot of hunters use crossbows."

"I'm not saying he was the one who shot at us, but I think he might be connected to the person who did. Like maybe it was one of the men in the picture or maybe he's friends with someone who wasn't in the picture. I don't know." She shrugged. "Could be he just knows him and they're friends but doesn't have any idea his friend is a killer."

"But what reason would said friend have to come after you?" Katherine asked.

Her head started to pound. "I don't know. I really don't know. It's so very con-fusing." She rubbed her eyes. "But they were looking for something, and I think the guy that was giving Dr. Rhodes a hard time wanted Rhodes to find it."

"But he hadn't."

"No." She waved a hand. "Hence the break-in."

"Then we need to ask Dr. Rhodes who he was talking to."

She nodded. That would fall under his responsibility. "Any word on the autopsy?" she asked Creed. "I need to know when they'll release her—" she couldn't bring herself to say *body* "—so that I know when to schedule the funeral."

"Yeah, the ME promised to get it done tomorrow."

"Good." On the one hand, she wasn't in a hurry to say her final goodbyes to Fawn, and yet she was. The funeral would bring closure. Not like finding her killer would bring, but it would help.

Lacey's phone rang and she snatched it from her back pocket. "It's Miranda."

"See what she wants," he said. "I'm going to make some calls of my own while you talk to her."

"And I'm going to head home," Katherine said. "I'll let myself out."

Lacey nodded. "Thank you for the food and everything."

"Of course. We'll talk later."

Lacey swiped the screen just before the call would go to voice mail and lifted the device to her ear. "Hi, Miranda."

"Lacey, I'm glad I caught you. I just wanted to check in with you and see if you'd made any progress in finding Fawn's killer?"

"Some. Hold on a second." She paused and walked into the kitchen, where she pulled her AirPods from the charger and slipped them into her ears. Might as well be productive while she talked. "I'm glad you called. I have a quick question for you."

"Sure."

"Do you think it's possible Dr. Rhodes could be the man Fawn was involved with?" Silence from the other end of the line echoed back at her. "Miranda?"

"Oh, sorry. Where did you get his name?"

"From one of the other doctors we talked to at the hospital. She never said the two of them were romantically involved, but as close as they were, he seemed like a good candidate. When we went to see him at his office, he had a lot of family and friends pictures on the credenza behind his desk. Fawn was in several of them. Of course, it could all be completely innocent. I don't want to say anything without evidence to back it up."

"That's good. No need to stir that pot."

"Do you think you could ask Tucker if he knows anything about who she might have been seeing? I mean, he and the doctor run with a pretty tight-knit group. Maybe one of them knows something?"

"I don't really think anything will come of it, but, sure, I can ask Tucker."

"Thank you."

"I mean, I knew Fawn and Dr. Rhodes were friends, but I can't really see him cheating on his wife. Like you said, he and Tucker are friends, and Tucker's never said a word about any sign of infidelity."

And the truth was, if Tucker knew the doctor was cheating, he might keep his mouth shut about it and Miranda would never know. "Considering Tucker's past with our father, how did Tucker feel about Fawn and you being friends? I mean, Fawn said they got along because they both loved you, but deep down, she said he still harbored resentment toward her."

Silence once more. "You're not accusing Tucker of anything, are you?"

"What? No. Not at all. But you were there when he screamed at Fawn and me in front of the whole school cafeteria. Was he still angry with Fawn?" *And me?*

"Absolutely not. He's gotten past all of that. It took some time and counseling, but he came to realize that you and Fawn had nothing to do with your father's actions. He and I were Fawn's friends. We often had dinner together and Fawn would come spend holidays with us when she wasn't with you." A lengthy pause stretched until Miranda said, "You didn't know all that."

"No." Wow. Had she known Fawn at all? "I see. Well, thank you for filling me in."

"Is everything okay, Lacey? Besides the obvious, I mean."

Lacey told the woman about the trashing of Fawn's home.

"Oh no, Lacey, I'm so sorry. Can I do anything to help?"

"No, but thanks."

"Okay, well, keep me updated on the investigation, will you? I can't stand that someone did this to her."

"Of course."

Lacey hung up and went to work on cleaning the rest of the kitchen. She and Katherine had gotten the worst of it, but there were still areas that could use some scrubbing.

A noise behind her spun her around. Creed stood in the doorway. "You okay?" he asked.

"Yeah." She told him about her conversation with Miranda. "I think we should have another talk with the doctor and straight up ask him if he was having an affair with Fawn." She couldn't believe those words were coming out of her mouth. "I also want to know who he was talking to in his office, what they're looking for and if he trashed my—*Fawn's*—house."

"I'm going to try to get ahold of Dr. Rhodes. If I can't, I'll get Ben to go find him. He also brought me some things, so I'm going to grab those. I can keep an eye on the house while he and I talk."

"Anything I need to know about?"

"He brought the papers for you to sign, since we can't seem to get that done."

"Oh. Right."

"Second thoughts?"

"No. My boss knows I'm going to be gone for a while." She shot him a smile. "One of the perks of working all the time is that I have tons of leave built up, and he's a compassionate guy. He knows I need to take care of Fawn's arrangements and...stuff."

Creed nodded.

"All right. I'm just going to be right outside. Call or text me if you need anything."

"I'll be fine, but thanks. I think I'm going to do some more searching and see what I can find. And probably some more cleaning."

"I can help you when I'm finished. Be right back. Lock the door behind me."

"Yes, sir." She saluted.

He rolled his eyes and stepped out onto the porch. "I'll be back."

"I'll probably be here."

With another eye roll, he shut the door behind him.

Scarlett nudged her hand. "I know, girl. Come on and I'll let you out the back and you can take care of business."

While Scarlett was outside in the fenced area, Lacey headed upstairs. The two bedrooms were almost finished but needed painting. Then she could get the furniture out of storage and—

What was she thinking? She didn't need the furniture that was in storage because she wasn't planning on staying here. She could sell the stuff and then the house once it was completed. She drew in a deep breath. "Okay, so that's the plan," she muttered. "Find Fawn's killer, have the funeral, finish fixing up the house and put it on the market."

The thought of burying her sister grieved her like nothing else. Not even her father's crimes or her breakup with Creed—although that came close. But what surprised her was the sadness that overwhelmed her when she thought about putting the house on the market.

"Why does that make me sad?" she whispered. "I'm so weird."

But it was definitely something to think about.

Creed slipped into the passenger seat next to Ben and leaned his head back. His side throbbed and he should probably take some more pain meds, but for now, he needed information Ben had. And the overnight bag. His mom had provided a change of clothes, but he needed a razor and a few other items. Ben handed him the bag. "What'd you find out?"

"Got the footage from the gym's camera.

You wouldn't believe the fuss the owner put up."

"Probably afraid he's going to be sued or something. And?"

"Parking-lot camera shows him following you and Lacey into the parking lot."

Creed frowned. "How'd I miss that?"

"I don't know. He didn't get out of his car right away, and when he did, he never showed his face."

"Plates?"

"He parked so the plates weren't facing the camera."

"So, he knew where the cameras were."

"Absolutely. That's even more evident as the footage plays. The guy gets out of the car and already has his hoodie pulled up. He went around to the side of the gym and entered on the west end."

Creed raised a brow. "He has a key to the gym?"

"That was my first thought, too," Ben said, "but no, members can use their card to scan in and bypass the front desk."

"Then they should have a record of the entry."

"Yep."

"So, who was it?"

"Gillian Fields."

Creed scoffed. "That wasn't Gillian Fields who attacked Lacey. The guy was big, muscled and mean."

"I know. I know Gillian, and when I talked to her, she said she lost her card and hasn't gotten a new one yet because she keeps thinking it's going to show up."

"When did she lose it?"

"The day Lacey was attacked."

Creed frowned. "Wait a minute. We had no idea that we would be visiting the gym. That was strictly a spur-of-the-moment thing. We went straight from Miranda's."

"Then someone knew you'd wind up there eventually?"

"No." He shook his head. "There's a connection to this Gillian Fields and whoever followed us to the gym."

"What kind of connection?"

"Someone with access to her purse keys."

He nodded. "All right. I'll talk to her again."

"And Miranda Glenn was the only one who knew we were going to the gym."

"I'll see if she said anything to anyone."

"Thanks, Ben. Now, what about Fawn's mail service? Did she stop it?"

"She didn't."

"So, she was coming here to get it or...?"

"No idea. We're still looking into that."

Creed looked around. The nearest neighbor in sight of Fawn's mailbox was about a quarter of a mile away. Properties in this area were spread out, but they were there. "Okay, the only way to get to this mailbox is to turn on Hillside Road. You'd pass six houses before getting back here to Fawn's. Let's see if anyone noticed a strange car—or maybe even a familiar one—driving this way over the past three months. It might not have been every day, maybe just a couple of times a week, but surely, someone saw something. Fawn's property is a dead end."

"Good point. I'll see if I can run that down."

"Good. I'm ready to find this person and put them away for good."

Creed's phone buzzed. His mother. He frowned and tapped the screen. "Hi, Mom."

"Someone broke into the store, Creed!" His mother's sob nearly tore him in two.

"Mom, stop. Tell me what happened."

"Your father had closed the store early and was doing the monthly inventory when someone kicked in the door. They punched him in the face, grabbed the cash on the counter and ran out the door."

Creed's stomach dipped. "I'll be on the way shortly, Mom. I just need to make sure Lacey's safe before I can leave. Is Dad okay?"

Ben looked at him. Creed muted the phone. "Call Mac and tell him to get out here. Then call Lacey and let her know to hunker down with her gun until Mac gets here. I need you to take me to the store—or the hospital. Not sure which just yet."

Ben grabbed his phone and punched the screen.

"The paramedics are here with him now," his mother was saying. "He...he has a b-broken nose and a fractured cheek, but they said he'll be fine. But he might need surgery."

His heart pounded. "Hang tight, Mom. I'll be there as fast as I can." He turned back to Ben. "Where's Mac?"

"On the way. He'll be here in ten minutes. Regina is on her way to the store. She said for you to stay with your parents."

"Lacey?"

"I'm guessing it won't take her that long to get out here."

He was right. The door to the house flew open and she ran to the car. Ben rolled the window down.

"Creed, are they okay?"

"Yes, but I need to get to them."

"Of course you do. Go."

"I'm not leaving you alone. Mac is on the way."

"I'll be fine. Now go."

"Get back in the house and lock the door. Then let me know when Mac gets here."

"I will. Give them my love."

He nodded and she darted back into the house. Creed glanced at his phone. A text from Zeb, the coroner. I managed to get to Fawn Jefferson's autopsy earlier than expected. I'll send you the report. Call me if you have questions.

Five more minutes and Mac would be there—and Lacey was armed. He nodded to Ben and they whipped out of Lacey's drive to head toward town.

FOURTEEN

Lacey's phone buzzed with a text. Mac had arrived and was parked on the curb. She walked to the window and waved at him. He waved back, and she turned, pressed fingers to her eyes, then dropped her hands and returned to the guest room.

This was where Fawn had planned to spend time working. She'd already painted two walls. The paint can sat to the left of the closet, and Lacey decided she might as well finish the other two. Maybe the mindless activity would help her gather her thoughts, go over the evidence in her head and figure out what she—and everyone else—was missing. And she could pray for Creed's father.

Scarlett joined her in the room and settled on the floor to watch her. "So, the paint is here, but where are the brushes?" The dog yawned and closed her eyes. "Well, you're a big help."

Lacey went to the guest room closet and opened the door. She'd glimpsed inside in her earlier search, but now started pulling things out. It wasn't a huge closet, but it had a lot of stuff. Well organized and neat, but packed. And she wanted to know what was in here. A few clothes hung on the bars and three cleaned paintbrushes sat on the shelf to her right, along with a drop cloth and several rags. Good to know. She'd come back to those.

Finally, she had everything out, including suitcases.Fawn had piled several blankets over something in the corner, a stack of pillows in front of them. And while Lacey had noticed this in her earlier search, she hadn't realized it was more than just a pile of blankets. Now she caught a glimpse of something behind the top pillow. She moved it and sucked in a breath. A two-drawer file cabinet.

Had her sister hidden it on purpose? Or was it just a convenient place to stack things when one had a lot of stuff to store? She pulled on the top drawer.

Locked.

Lacey spun, raced to grab the keys she'd found in the gym bag and hurried back. The second key slid home and she opened the drawer.

Files upon files.

She opened the bottom drawer. The same, only it was half-full. A large bag took up the other half of the drawer.

"Okay, then," she told Scarlett, "looks like our plans have changed. The painting is going to have to wait."

It took her four trips, but she pulled every file from the drawer and set everything in the corner of the room. She dropped the bag next to the nearest stack and settled herself on the floor in front of it. She started with the stack of files to her left. Car insurance, home warranty, various receipts from the renovation, a life insurance policy with Lacey as the beneficiary for almost half a million dollars.

Lacey nearly choked. "Oh, Fawn..." she whispered. The bag kept snagging her attention, so she opened it. And found cash. A *lot* of cash. Lacey pulled it all out with shaking fingers and counted it. Twenty thousand dollars. "What in the world, Fawn?" Maybe it was simply some kind of emergency stash.

But...for what? She snapped pictures of it, then stuffed it all back in the bag and zipped it shut. She went back to the files, hoping she would find something that would give her a clue about the money. She found the bank statements and eagerly scanned them, looking for the large withdrawal.

But even going back a full year, there was nothing.

Could Fawn have another account she didn't know about? Probably not. She had a checking account and a savings account.

Time passed, and when she looked up, it

was dark outside. She shot a text to Creed.
How are your parents?

His reply came back shortly.

At the hospital with Dad. He's going to be
okay. A broken nose, but no surgery required. His cheekbone is fractured, so he'll
have to be careful not to do any more damage, but he'll be going home shortly and
I'll head back to your place to relieve Mac.

Did you catch the guy who did it?

Not yet, but Dad has more cameras than
the average store. Regina's already started
going through the footage.

Can I help?

No, the best thing you can do is stay put
and stay safe. Please, Lacey.

She grimaced. I'm staying put. Found
some more files in the guest closet, so
going through those.

Good. Let me know if you find anything.

I found something, but not sure how it relates. It's a bag of cash. I also found her bank statements, but nothing to indicate that she withdrew a large amount of cash in the last year. No idea where it came from. I found her life insurance policy and other pertinent documents.

She set her phone aside and sighed.

Scarlett had started pacing, her gaze swinging toward the door, then back to Lacey. "Need to go out, girl?"

Scarlett raced for the stairs. Lacey let her out, filled the dog's bowls, then returned to the room. The next file she found was labeled Medical.

Lacey went to the chair and opened the folder on the desk under the lamp. The first thing she saw was a medical bill for a gynecologist in South Carolina. But it was the copy of an ultrasound picture that sent shards of shock shivering through her. F. Miller. Then it had the date of the ultrasound and the fact that the woman was eight weeks pregnant.

The air left her lungs and she wilted even while her mind quickly did the math. The baby would be a couple of weeks old if she had carried it full term. Older if she'd delivered early.

Lacey quickly flipped through more pictures. Two months later, at sixteen weeks, there was another ultrasound. This one confirmed it was a boy. And this was another copy of the original. So where were the originals?

And the next five pictures, from a private imaging company located five hours away—why so far?—showed the baby in full 3D at seven and a half months. Lacey gasped. He was beautiful. Perfect in every way. Who was he? Why did Fawn have pictures of another woman's ultrasound? She traced a finger over the little hand. All four fingers and his tiny thumb, spread like he was waving at her. Another picture showed him yawning. In the next, he was sucking his thumb.

Lacey swallowed hard and texted Creed. I found ultrasound pictures in Fawn's filing cabinet. The woman's name on them is F. Miller. Miller was their mother's maiden name.

Her phone rang and she snatched it up. "Creed?"

"Are you sitting down?"

"Just tell me."

"I just read the autopsy report. I was getting ready to call you when I got your text."

"Okay." She could barely breathe, scared of what he had to say and wanting to shake him for not saying it faster. "What?"

"Fawn recently either *had* a baby or lost one."

"What?" Lacey let out a laugh of disbelief. "No, she didn't."

"Autopsy says she did." He paused while Lacey's brain scrambled for words. "I think those pictures may be of Fawn's child," he finally said. "It makes sense."

"No. That's impossible."

"Lacey—"

"She would have told me." Her words sounded strained and desperate even to her own ears.

"She might not have, Lacey. If she was pregnant by a married man—"

"But why use a different name?" F. Miller. Fawn Miller?

"To make sure no one discovered whatever deception she was involved with. A nonprofit pregnancy center would do the ultrasounds for free. What's the name of the clinic?"

"Harrisburg Women's Clinic."

"Hold on." Seconds later, he said, "Yeah, it's a free clinic."

Could it be? "Miller is my mom's maiden name, Creed. I think you might be right." Her heart squeezed. "It's a boy," she said around a tight throat. "She had a son if she gave birth and he wasn't stillborn or anything."

"Look for adoption papers."

"I've been through almost all of the files. There aren't any adoption papers so far."

"Okay, one more thing and this is going to hurt."

"Tell me."

"Zeb said the first blow to Fawn's head didn't kill her." Lacey stifled a gasp. "Her hyoid bone was broken."

"She was *strangled*? Oh, Creed, no..." Tears overflowed to drip off her chin. She sniffed and wiped them away. "Finish telling me, please. All of it."

"Zeb said the bruises on her throat indicate that someone held an object there. Whoever did it didn't use his hands, so there's no prints. Most likely, it was a piece of wood or something."

A sob slipped from her.

"I'm so sorry, Lacey."

She drew in a steadying breath. She could cry and grieve later. Voices in the background reached her while her mind spun with the new information. Her sister had been strangled.

"Hang on a sec again," he said.

She held, fighting tears and a dark fury at the person who'd done this to her sister.

Strangled. She was still trying to wrap her mind around it when he came back on the line. "I've got to go," he said, "but I won't be much longer. There's nothing I can do here. Dad's going to be okay, so I'll be heading back your way shortly."

"Okay. Thank you."

"I know this is a shock, Lacey. We'll process it together when I get back."

"Yeah."

"'Bye."

She hung up and pressed shaking fingers to her lips. "Oh, Fawn, I'm so sorry. Where's your baby?" Had she miscarried? Had he been stillborn and Fawn had needed time to heal and process? But the timeline didn't work. Fawn would have taken her three-month sabbatical around her sixth month of pregnancy. Meaning she planned to give birth, then go back to work.

After she gave the baby up for adoption?

She wasn't planning to keep him, as there was nothing in the house that even hinted there was a child coming. Then again, maybe she had put everything in storage? But that made absolutely no sense. Fawn wouldn't have been fixing up the house and not have had a nursery ready for her child if she'd planned on keeping him.

A noise from downstairs stiffened her spine until she remembered she'd let Scarlett out and the dog probably wanted back in. She ran down the steps and opened the door and Scarlett brushed past her. Lacey shut the door and hurried back up the stairs, only to stop and sniff. Gasoline?

Scarlett barked. Then barked a never-ending sound that said she wasn't happy.

Lacey's phone buzzed from the guest room and she raced to retrieve it. A text from Mac. Stay inside. Someone just tossed liquid onto your front porch. I'm going after him.

Fury stiffened her spine and she snagged her weapon from the floor near the stack of files. She dialed Mac's number, and it rang four times, then went to voice mail.

With a groan, she called Creed.

As soon as he picked up, she said, "Someone's here. Mac's not answering his phone and I smell—" A loud crash, the breaking of glass, and a whoosh came from the first floor, sending her scrambling down the stairs. Scarlett's barking took on a new edge of frantic.

"Scarlett!"

"Lacey!" Creed's shout shook her out of her panic even as she stared at the wall of flames lining the front of the house.

Another crash from the kitchen.

"Creed, the house is on fire!" She ran toward the sound and stopped as soon as she came to the entrance to the kitchen. Flames were already licking quickly in her direction. Two more booms from the den spun her. Scarlett bounded to her, barking and spinning. Lacey jammed her gun into her waistband and grabbed the dog's collar with her free hand, her heart pounding. "I'm trapped, Creed! Someone threw Molotov cocktails inside. At least three, maybe more!"

Smoke lodged in her lungs and she coughed.

She heard him giving Ben orders to call for help. "I'm on the way!"

"Check on Mac. He's not answering." She had to get away from the smoke— and the paint cans before they exploded. Coughing, she and Scarlett bolted upstairs to the guest room. Already the smoke was swirling in the room and the smoke alarm blared. Lacey shut the door behind her, dragged in a lungful of clean air, then raced to the closet to snag two pillows. She stuffed them against the crack left between the door and the floor.

"Lacey! Talk to me!"

She just realized Creed was yelling at her on the phone. "I'm in my old room. I'm going to be in our spot and will need a ladder to get down!"

"Fire truck is on the way. Hold tight."

Like she had a choice.

Scarlett whined and backed away from the door. Smoke continued to fill the room in spite of her best efforts to stop it with the pillows. She went to the window and opened it. Cold air rushed in and smoke billowed out, but she was able to grab another gasp of pure night air.

She glanced back at the bedroom door. The pillows were burning. Lacey grabbed the bag of money and the medical file with the ultrasound pictures. She shoved them out the window and climbed after them, planting her feet securely on the roof. "Scarlett, come."

The dog hesitated. Then, with trust in her eyes, she followed Lacey out the window. Lacey kept a tight hold on the animal's collar with one hand and shut the window with the other. Grateful for a pocket of fresh air, she looked in the direction of town and could see the flashing red lights of the fire trucks and blue lights of the law enforcement vehicles.

But what about Mac? *Oh, please, God, let Mac be all right.* "I'm out on the roof, Creed. I have Scarlett with me."

"I'm just a few minutes away."

"Please check on Mac. I haven't seen or heard from him. I'm worried for him."

"We'll check on him. You just concentrate on staying alive."

As the flames licked closer, she wondered if the person after her would finally win.

Creed left his parents in the good and caring hands of some friends from their church and headed as fast as he dared toward Lacey's home. Ten minutes later, Ben was turning into her drive, and the sight that greeted him made him nauseous.

The fire trucks had arrived ahead of them and already had the hoses aimed at the burning home. Another truck was backing toward the window that used to be Lacey's old room. Creed couldn't see her, thanks to the thick smoke, but he pictured her and Scarlett on the roof, waiting for the ladder to reach the edge. *Please, God, get her down safe.*

Ben pulled to a stop next to Mac's car and threw the cruiser in Park. "You check on Mac," Creed said. "I'm going after Lacey."

Ben headed for Mac, and Creed sent up a silent prayer for the man while he aimed himself toward the back of the house.

"Lacey?" His shout turned several heads, but the truck was there and the ladder was almost in place. He looked up and Lacey's gaze locked on his.

"Creed?" Creed turned to see Parker Adams, the fire chief, coming toward him. "What are you doing here?"

"Lacey called me."

"We're trying to get her down. She refuses to come down until the dog is safe, but apparently the dog is being skittish and my guy can't get close enough to grab her. And Lacey isn't strong enough to force her."

"Scarlett knows me. Let me try."

"Yeah, fine. Just hurry. The fire is burning hot and getting closer to her."

Creed ran to the ladder, grabbed the face mask someone held out to him, then hurried up the stairs to come face-to-face with a struggling Lacey. She coughed and her eyes and nose streamed from the smoke.

"Give me Scarlett!"

"Scarlett, go."

The dog hesitated.

"Come here, girl," Creed said. "Scarlett, come."

Another coughing fit shook Lacey. Scarlett barked and took a few steps closer to Creed. That was all he needed. He lunged forward and grabbed the dog's collar. Scarlett balked at first, but Creed was stronger and he soon had her in his arms. He turned and passed her to the firefighter behind him.

Smoke swirled, flames shot from the roof toward the sky and a loud crack echoed around them. The roof started to collapse, and Lacey screamed even as she catapulted toward him. Creed caught her with one arm. Fire of a different kind arched through his stitched side, but he held on to Lacey with his left arm and clung to the ladder with his right. She swung below him, legs pumping air. "Grab the ladder,

Lacey!" He was going to drop her if she didn't do something. And fast.

She must have heard the desperation in his tone, because she launched herself toward the nearest rung and hooked her elbow around it. "I got it," she rasped.

"Hang on!"

"I can't."

"You can. I'll help you, but you've got to pull yourself around in front of me. We'll go down together."

"Creed…"

"Now, Lacey!"

She groaned, and he grabbed a handful of her T-shirt, and with his help, she maneuvered herself around to the right side of the ladder. Creed sucked in a breath and grimaced at the agony shooting in his side, but began the descent. One rung at a time.

When they reached the bottom, Scarlett barked, frantic to get to her. "Let her go," Lacey said. The firefighter did and Scarlett hurtled herself at Lacey. "Good girl. Sit."

Scarlett sat. Lacey looked up at Creed. "Got a rope? Her lead is toast."

"No, but we'll find one. Now come on. You need oxygen."

He led Lacey to the back of the ambulance, and Annie slapped a mask over her face. "Scarlett, down. Settle." At Lacey's hoarse command, Scarlett dropped on the floor beside the gurney, eyes watching everything, nose twitching, sides heaving with her pants.

Annie and Hannah were once again the paramedics on call. Annie placed a dog oxygen mask over Scarlett's snout and Creed was surprised the animal didn't try to shake it off.

Lacey looked at Creed and pulled the oxygen mask away. "Mac?"

"I'm going to go find out. Be right back."

Creed left her and jogged back to the car where he found Ben soaking wet and passing a bottle of water to an equally saturated Mac. Mac blinked up at them, his eyes foggy.

"What happened?" Creed asked.

"Found him on the ground around the side of the house," Ben said. "He was hidden by the bushes, but the hoses got us."

"I saw someone sneaking around," Mac said, "and went after them. Whoever it was got the drop on me." He pressed a hand to his bleeding head. "Man. That smarts." His eyes sharpened and homed in on Creed. "Lacey?"

"She's okay. Some smoke inhalation, but nothing she can't recover from."

Mac's face reflected his relief. "I'm sorry, man."

"Don't worry about it. You can ride in the ambulance with Lacey to the hospital."

"No, I'm okay."

"As your boss, I'm telling you to get checked out."

"Gotcha."

Creed and Ben helped Mac to the ambulance. "Got another rider for you."

"Mac," Lacey said. "You're okay." She blinked back tears when Mac climbed inside and sat on the floor. "I was so worried about you." Creed's heart tumbled over itself at the fact that she cared so much for the safety of his friend when she'd just lost her childhood home and barely escaped with her life.

"Yeah." Mac groaned and leaned his head back. "I'm so sorry, Lacey. I can't tell you how sorry I am."

"It's just a house, Mac. We're alive, and I'm grateful."

Mac squeezed her hand and Creed looked on. "I'm right behind you two. See you at the hospital."

He shut the door and turned to give orders to Ben. "Get a crime scene unit here and the arson unit from Asheville. This guy had to have left some kind of evidence behind, and I want it found before it's too late."

FIFTEEN

At the hospital, Lacey was diagnosed with mild smoke inhalation, but there'd be no permanent damage. Fortunately, she'd managed to get to clean air fast enough, and after medications and oxygen treatments, she was feeling much better. Katherine stopped in with orders to rest and the key to her former apartment located above the local medical clinic. "It's furnished, but because no one's lived there in a while, I've called in a cleaning crew. By the time you get there, it should be in order."

Lacey took the key with a tight throat—more from her emotions than the smoke—and nodded her thanks. Then frowned. "A cleaning crew? At this time of night?"

Katherine winked. "They're a special

kind of crew. You're staying here for the night, but the apartment will be ready for you around ten in the morning."

"Thank you, Katherine," she whispered. Then cleared her throat, grateful that it was only a tad sore. "How's Mac?"

"Slight concussion but heading home to Isabelle to rest."

"He'll have the next few days off to heal," Creed said. He'd been sitting silently in the chair near the window.

Lacey turned to look at him, noting the pained creases in his forehead and his hand pressed to his side. "Did you get checked out?"

"I'm fine."

Lacey simply turned her eyes to Katherine, who raised a brow at Creed.

Creed sighed and pulled his shirt up to reveal he'd ripped his stitches loose. Katherine shook her head. "You two are going to have quite the story to tell your kids one day."

Lacey froze and Creed stilled.

Katherine flushed. "I mean, not *your*

kids as in your kids together, but just *your* kids. If you have any with other— Okay, I'm going to stop now and go get a suture kit to fix that wound. Be right back."

She was out the door before Lacey could blink. Then she laughed. And coughed. And laughed some more. Creed looked at her with concern. "You okay?"

"Yes." She wiped her watering eyes. "Sorry. I guess it wasn't that funny. Maybe I just needed the release of laughter, which has been sorely missing from my life lately." She took another hit of oxygen and caught her breath. Thankful to be feeling better, she tried to ignore the fact she was so tired, she could barely keep her eyes open. Then she remembered the bag and sat up with a gasp. "Where's the stuff I threw down out of the window? The bag?"

"It's at the office with Ben."

She flopped back with a relieved sigh. "Good."

"No idea where she got the money?" he asked.

"No. Not a clue." She bit her lip. "And

the autopsy showed she was pregnant. I can't even…"

"Yeah."

Lacey nodded. "I guess we can make an educated guess as to what she was doing those three months."

"She was hiding her pregnancy."

"From me and everyone else." She shook her head. "So, where's her baby?"

"From the way people have described her, it sounds like she could have lost him."

"Yes." She'd thought of that.

"Or," he said, "maybe she gave him up for adoption. Maybe she took the time to work through all that comes with that."

"Possibly." Lacey yawned and forced her eyes back open. She frowned. "No, wait. The dates from the ultrasound and her leave of absence would put her going back to work a week after she gave birth. Unless she had him early or something."

He ran his hand through his hair. "So, she finds out she's pregnant. The father is likely the mysterious doctor she'd been seeing—possibly Dr. Rhodes. Maybe she told him she was pregnant and he didn't want anything to do with that."

"Maybe the twenty grand was a payoff of some sort?" Lacey asked. "His altruistic gesture that says, 'I don't want the child, but I'm not a bad guy. Here's money to take care of you and the baby for a while.'"

He nodded. "And maybe Fawn felt like she couldn't raise the child on her own— or she just didn't want him."

"She'd want him." Lacey breathed deeply from the oxygen mask. The talking was hurting her throat, but she *had* to figure this out. "Or maybe she wouldn't." She threw her hands up. "I have no idea at this point. Mostly because I have to admit that I have no idea who Fawn was." The thought made her want to cry. She'd thought she and Fawn were close, but by Lacey keeping her distance, it had been a false closeness. Add in Fawn hiding secrets and keeping Lacey in the dark about her personal issues and troubles and...yeah.

"You knew her," Creed said. "You just didn't know all her secrets. The sister you knew and loved was still there. Just because she withheld this from you doesn't mean she was some stranger."

"Well, she feels like it."

He sighed. "I know. I'm sorry." He rose to kiss her forehead and Lacey's heart nearly jumped out of her chest. When he drew back, his gaze met hers and she couldn't decipher the look.

"Creed—"

"Get some rest, Lacey. There's a guard on the door. I'm going to check on my dad. Then I'll be back to stay in that surprisingly comfortable chair the rest of the night."

"Oh, Creed, you don't have to—"

"And then I'll take you home—well, to Katherine's old place—in the morning and we'll get a fresh start on looking into Fawn's pregnancy and who might have known about it, why she felt the need to keep it a secret, where the money came from, and so on. And I'm going to call Dr. Rhodes right now and ask him if the baby is his."

"I must be a bad influence," she murmured. "You just interrupted me twice."

He chuckled, and Lacey let her eyelids flutter shut. She was too tired to think straight, but because Creed was by her side, she'd be able to sleep.

On the way home from the hospital the next morning, Creed finally got ahold of Dr. Rhodes. He hesitated a moment, then put the phone on speaker so Lacey could hear. "Thank you for taking my call."

"I suppose this is about Fawn?"

"It is. I'm just going to come right out and ask you. Did you have an affair with her?"

A heavy sigh filtered through the line. "Yes. I did."

Lacey gave a small gasp, then pressed her fingers to her lips.

"Did you know she was pregnant?"

A long pause. Creed glanced at Lacey. "Dr. Rhodes?"

"Yes. I knew," he finally said.

"And did you give her twenty thousand dollars?"

"Well, you've really done your homework, haven't you?" His low voice filtered through the line, a combination of weariness and hesitancy...and maybe a fraction of relief mixed in. "I did. I told her whatever she decided about the child was her decision, but I could have no part in its life."

"What was her reaction to that?"

"She was hurt, but she understood. We never sugarcoated what we were doing and neither of us had blinders on. Fawn never asked me to leave my family for her and I never offered. But...it wasn't a fling. It wasn't a one-night stand. I loved Fawn."

"But you tried to pay her off to get rid of the baby."

"Yes." His sigh echoed through the line. "I did. I'm not proud of it, but I didn't kill her."

"Why didn't you just come clean when we asked you?"

"Because I was scared. Scared because,

in your eyes, it would give me a motive to kill her. And I didn't, but I couldn't figure out if I had an alibi or not."

"I'm going to need one."

"I know. Give me the day and time you need one for and I'll find a way to provide it."

Creed told him and the man promised to get back to him. "One more question. Lacey overheard a conversation between you and someone in your office about you needing to find something or you would be in trouble. Who were you talking to?"

"She heard that?"

"She did."

"That was Dr. Fitzgerald. Some data on our project was misplaced and it could have ruined the entire thing. All that hard work down the drain. I was devastated. But we wound up finding it, so everything worked out."

"I see. You know I'll be talking to Dr. Fitzgerald."

"Of course. Talk to him. I have six other doctors who can back that up."

"Thank you, Dr. Rhodes." He hung up and Creed asked Ben to keep an eye on the man. "Watch him. If he tries to run, arrest him."

"On it."

He was going to have so much overtime to pay out this month.

Creed shot Lacey a glance. "Well, that answers a few questions. We're getting closer."

"Yeah." She wiped a stray tear and sniffed. Then straightened her shoulders and pulled in a deep breath.

Creed spun into the medical facility parking lot and parked. He climbed carefully out of the driver's seat with his hand pressed to his side. This time, he'd refused all drugs that might keep him from driving. Together, he, Scarlett and Lacey walked up the steps, and he pushed open the door, holding it for Lacey and Scarlett. As soon as they stepped inside, he followed and could smell someone had been doing some deep cleaning.

Lacey sniffed. "Wow."

Katherine came out of the kitchen, followed by Miranda, Jessica Hill, Annie, the paramedic, and two other ladies. "Surprise," Katherine said.

Lacey let out a low laugh. "The cleaning crew?"

Katherine nodded. "Just finished up."

Miranda walked over and hugged Lacey. "I'm so glad you're okay."

"Me, too," Jessica said.

Annie replaced Miranda and gave Lacey a quick squeeze. "We all are."

"You guys..." Lacey swallowed and a tear dripped down her cheek. "I don't even know what to say."

"Try 'thank you,'" Creed said.

She elbowed him in his good side. A light tap that would have had more force behind it if he hadn't been injured. "Thank you," Lacey said. "From the bottom of my heart, thank you." She walked into the den area. "Oh, look, a bed for Scarlett right there in front of the fireplace." She pressed her hands against her chest as though her emotions were too much. She turned back to the group watching, then looked at Scarlett and pointed. "Scarlett, bed."

Scarlett loped over and made herself comfortable on the oversize cushion. The ladies laughed and Jessica clapped. "She loves it."

"Of course."

"All right," Katherine said, "you have a couple of weeks' worth of clothing hanging in the master closet, a few towels, a change of sheets and all that you should need for a comfy stay. Creed, we got some more clothes from your mom so you can have something that doesn't smell like smoke. There's enough dog food and treats for Scarlett that I should be her new BFF. Oh, and a well-stocked fridge, including a couple of casseroles you can heat and eat. Easy enough, right?"

"Oh my." Lacey shook her head, and Creed thought his heart would burst at the love being shown to this woman who thought everyone in town hated her. Who thought she *deserved* to be hated because of her father's actions.

Katherine gave her one more hug. "We're going to get out of here so you can get some rest."

"But before we do that," Jessica said, "I wanted to invite you to my baby shower."

Lacey raised a brow. "But you just had a baby."

"Yes, but the shower was rescheduled because I had her early. Please say you'll come if you feel like it. It's a drop-in, so you don't have to stay long if you don't want to, but I'd love to have you there. And don't worry about a gift. Just come."

"When?"

"Day after tomorrow."

"Um...yes, sure, I'll try."

"Well, it's at my house," Miranda said, "so leave the dog at home, okay?" She laughed. "Sorry, that sounded kind of rude. I didn't mean it that way."

Lacey gave her a gentle smile. "I didn't take it that way. Of course. I'll leave her here." She'd noticed Miranda staying away from Scarlett. "Bad experience with dogs?"

"Something like that." She clapped her hands. "Then I guess we'll see you at the shower. Feel better."

"Thank you."

Miranda turned and left, followed by the others echoing her well-wishes.

Soon, it was just Creed and Lacey left in the place, and he motioned for her to sit. "Relax. I'll fix some food and arrange for some security on this place."

She nodded. The fact that she didn't argue or offer to help told him an awful lot about her state of mind.

Once he'd fixed both of them a plate of chicken casserole, he carried it to the den, handed her the food and made himself comfortable on the couch. "I don't know about you, but I think the fire thing was a pretty desperate act."

"I know." Her brow remained furrowed.

"What are you thinking?"

"Just trying to fill in the puzzle. Someone was watching the house even before I came back."

"Yes, looks that way."

"I'm also convinced someone went through all of Fawn's drawers before they decided to be bold and just trash the place. I also think," she said slowly, "they didn't find what they were looking for, so they simply burned the house down. I'm not sure they were actually trying to kill me, but were more interested in getting rid of whatever it is they were looking for. Although, maybe killing me in the process could be considered a bonus. Who knows?"

"You think the person knew about the money and the ultrasound pictures?"

She nodded, then looked up and met his gaze. "I don't know about that, but it makes sense. More than that, though, I think that there was more than one person."

That stilled him. "Why do you say that?"

"Because the little cocktails came in the back and the front almost simultaneously."

"Well, it would explain how someone was able to sneak up behind Mac. If his attention was on one attacker, the other could have knocked him out." He paused. "I think the break-in at my parents' store was a distraction."

She raised a brow. "Why?"

"Because they needed Ben and me gone in order to get to you. The way to make that happen was to make the attack personal."

Lacey swallowed hard and shook her head. "Okay, if that's the case, then they probably didn't plan on Mac getting here quite so fast and decided to just take care of him when he went looking for them."

"Maybe. Or they figured one person would be easier to deal with than two. They might have thought I'd take off, leaving Ben alone to guard you. Either way, their plan worked to a certain extent. They only had to deal with one person."

She ate three bites, then set it aside. "It's good, but I'm about to fall asleep where I'm sitting. I'll eat after I take a nap. But before I find my way to the bed, I need to know if there's anything else the autopsy report came back with."

Creed sighed. "Nothing I haven't already told you. Just that she'd been pregnant—either having given birth to a live child or had a late-term miscarriage."

"And she was hit in the head with something that knocked her out and then someone strangled her while she was unconscious?"

"That's what it looks like, according to Zeb. There's no pattern to the head wound, no shards of wood or glass, just dirt. The kind of dirt that matched where she was buried."

"So no speculation about what the weapon was?"

He shook his head. "Zeb said he wasn't willing to make any guesses, but the weapon was probably something grabbed on the spur of the moment, something found around the house—which brings us back to a 'fit of rage' impulse killing, not a planned, premeditated thing."

"Okay. Thanks."

She stood and sniffed, and he had a feeling she was trying to hide the fact that she was crying. "I need a shower and a change of clothes," she said, her voice husky. "I think I'm going to go do that."

He rose, walked to her and pulled her into a hug. She wrapped her arms around his waist and sighed. Then stepped back as though lingering was against the rules. And, he supposed, it kind of was, based on their previous conversation. "Lacey..."

Her gaze met his. Tears were there, but she blinked them away. "Yes?"

"I'm glad you came back."

A small, sad smile curved her lips. "I... I...think I am, too, but..."

He closed the distance between them. Lowered his head but hesitated a fraction of an inch from her lips. If she wanted to push him away or step back, she could. But she didn't. She gripped his biceps to pull him nearer, and he settled his lips over hers, kissing her, reliving the past and hoping for a future with her. A sigh slipped from her and she slid her arms around his neck to thread her fingers through his hair. He deepened the kiss, hoping every emotion he couldn't seem to find the words for came through loud and clear.

And then it was over. He stepped back, his throat tight with longing and more words he wanted to say.

Lacey opened her eyes, more tears glinting in them. Then she rose up on her tiptoes to kiss him on the cheek. Without another word, she walked around him and headed toward what would be her bedroom tonight.

Creed settled on the sofa to keep watch over the woman he'd fallen in love with again.

Or maybe he'd never actually stopped loving her.

Whatever the case, he steeled himself against the familiar pain her leaving was going to bring him once again.

SIXTEEN

He didn't want her to go, but he didn't care enough to come with her. Same old, same old.

So...stay.

The voice inside her head nudged her and she shrugged it away.

The reason for leaving no longer exists.

"Stop it," she whispered.

But that kiss...

She groaned and slapped a hand to her head. "Don't think about it."

But how could she not?

Scarlett whined from her spot at the foot of the bed. Lacey walked over to scratch the dog's ears, then turned to pace the room, reliving the moment they'd kissed. It was like she'd never left. Like they'd never argued. Like they were going to be together forever.

But they weren't.

They *had* argued.

And she *had* left.

And he'd let her go.

"Arghhh!" The growl hurt her throat and sent her into a coughing spasm. She sipped on the bottle of water she'd found in the bathroom and caught her breath.

She'd take a shower, swallow some more meds and then have a nap. She went through the closet and the bathroom and found everything she needed for a shower, some shampoo and a change of clothes. The toothbrush and toothpaste were a much-appreciated added bonus.

Twenty minutes later, she was under the covers, her mind spinning once more with something triggered by Creed's statement and kiss—and the stunning thought that she wanted to stay. She had friends here who'd taken time to come help her. Friends she hadn't really counted as friends.

She sat up, overwhelmed with one thought.

"I shut everyone out," she murmured. "It's me." Every relationship she had was on her terms. Even the ones back in Charlotte. She was closer to her dogs than any of the people she would have called friends before this morning. Not that they weren't good people, but she'd never encouraged them to know her.

And, in spite of her "I have a great life in Charlotte" speech, it wouldn't bother her overly much to leave them all behind. *Why?*

Because deep down in her subconscious she'd known she'd want to come home one day? That she'd been clinging to the hope that Creed would call her and tell her that they'd work it out no matter the distance between them?

"No," she said. Scarlett lifted her head and looked at her. "It couldn't be that, could it, girl?"

Scarlett yawned and closed her eyes, but Lacey's stayed wide-open, sleep having fled. Had she really lived the last six years of her life with the hope that Creed would come after her?

No way.

Maybe.

Quite possibly.

Since her breakup with Creed, she'd not accepted one single date offer from anyone. There'd been several men who'd asked her out, and she always had an excuse why she couldn't go.

She sucked in a breath at her self-analysis and set off a coughing spasm. When her lungs calmed down, she rolled over and closed her eyes. *Take a nap, Lacey. It'll help.*

Not really thinking she'd sleep, she was shocked when she rolled over to look at her phone and saw two hours had passed. She rose, dressed in sweats, heavy socks and a long-sleeved T-shirt that smelled like vanilla and roses. She smiled. Katherine had donated this one. "Come on, girl," Lacey said to Scarlett. "Let's go get some food. And then we'll call the insurance company." The thought of all she needed to deal with was overwhelming, but it couldn't be helped.

When she walked into the den, she found Creed on the phone, his laptop open on the coffee table. He looked up and met her gaze. "Yeah, thanks," he said into the phone. "Got it. Talk to you in a little bit." He hung up and Lacey raised a brow. "Dr. Rhodes has an airtight alibi for Fawn's death. He was hunting with two of his buddies, and they have time-stamped videos of him celebrating the buck he bagged."

"So, he didn't kill her."

"No. He's most likely the baby's father, but he didn't kill her."

His eyes narrowed and Lacey gulped. *Please, please, please don't bring up that kiss.*

He didn't. Instead, he said, "How do you feel?"

"I'm all right. A little sore throat, scratchy lungs and a bit of a headache, but I'm breathing fine. Everything should clear up in a day or so."

"I'm glad." He sighed. "I was scared for you."

"I was scared for me, too." She nodded to his laptop. "You mind if I use that to order a baby gift for Jessica?"

He pushed it toward her. "Help yourself. Password is LaceyLeeJ100."

She froze, met his gaze and then sighed. "We're a pair, Creed Payne."

"I'm hoping."

She ignored the two words, not wanting to give him hope by telling him what she was thinking. If she decided to stay in Timber Creek, she had to be 100 percent sure that was what she wanted.

But she knew one thing: she desperately wanted to find a way to be with Creed for the rest of their lives.

But first, she needed a baby gift for the shower. "If I'm going to that baby shower, we need to make sure everything is safe for me to be there. I can't put anyone at risk."

Creed pursed his lips and nodded. "I get it. I don't think you'll be putting anyone at risk. The only people who've been in danger are you and me."

"What about Hank? You were holding him."

"And the bullets were aimed more at you. The bullets never came close to him."

"And being almost run over in the middle of the street?"

"Only you. Granted, the car could have hurt someone if he hadn't run into the concrete barrier, but he didn't."

"And while Ethan Mays could have been hurt, he wasn't anywhere near when the bolts came our way. He—or they—want me to be alone," she said slowly. "Although, they don't seem to mind you getting caught in the cross fire."

"But I put myself there. And they could have killed Mac but didn't."

"Why do you think?"

Creed drew in a breath. "Because whoever killed Fawn is the one after you. He needs you out of the way for a reason. He's not randomly killing people. As long as he—they—whoever—can't get to you, they'll wait and bide their time. But give them an opportunity and they're going to take it." He paused. "I'll go with you and watch the house. If I see anything that sets off my internal alarms, I'll let you know, and you can simply leave."

She nodded. "That works for me."

"For now, I have a couple of friends who are going to watch this place while we're here."

"Friends?"

"I don't have enough manpower. I won't leave you unprotected, but I've also got a town to keep up with. Regina and Ben are working overtime while Mac heals. I'd love two or three more deputies, but…" He shrugged. "Money." He kept his gaze on hers. "I need some help and I'm not too proud to ask for it. I have it in my budget for two more deputies. And one of those people has got to be the leader of the K-9 unit." And he wanted that person to be her.

She didn't look away. "I'm thinking about it. Seriously." Hope flared in his gaze and she snapped her lips shut. "But

I'm not making any promises. There's a lot to consider, so I'm not in a rush to make a decision, okay?"

"I understand." He paused. "But just in case you decide not to take the job, I have a list of candidates for you to look over. I need to have someone in mind and be ready to act when…if…you say no. Do you mind?"

"Of course not." A flicker of…something…ignited in her gut. She wasn't sure she could put a name to the feeling, but was very aware she didn't want anyone else starting the K-9 program. She wanted to do it. But Creed expected her to refuse.

For the next few hours, she sifted through the names and résumés that had already come in and found several applicants who would be perfect for the job.

Except they weren't.

Because they weren't her.

Two days later, Creed was still mulling over the fact that Lacey was thinking about taking the job. His heart beat faster just knowing she wasn't turning him down cold. She wanted to stay. He could see it in her eyes.

But what if she chose not to?

He ran a hand over his head and down his cheek. He'd borrowed her shower once again but hadn't bothered to shave. For now, he was making plans to keep Lacey safe while she attended the baby shower.

Two of his buddies from the Asheville Police Department had agreed to guard the apartment for the last two days, and all had been quiet, but they'd left and now it was up to him, Ben and Regina to watch out for Lacey.

He'd also learned that the break-in at his parents' store very well could have been a distraction to get him away from Lacey's home so the person could make his move to burn her home to the ground.

Who else would know about the baby? The ultrasound pictures? The money? Who would willingly burn up twenty thousand dollars in cash?

Someone who didn't need it?

Someone who thought it could be traced back to them?

Someone who didn't know it was there and thought they were just going to kill Lacey for whatever reason?

The questions spun through his mind with no answers in sight.

Lacey walked into the den and his heart did that flip-flop thing it had done ever since he'd seen her in the middle school cafeteria. It had taken a while to work up the nerve to ask her out. When she'd said yes, he'd been over the moon.

And then she'd walked away six years into their relationship.

At least now he knew she'd looked back while doing so.

"You look great," he said.

"Thanks. I hope they don't mind casual. My wardrobe is pretty limited."

"I think they'll understand."

"Yes."

"One thing. When I talked to Dr. Rhodes about his alibi, he mentioned his wife was going to be at the shower. He asked me to ask you not to say anything about the affair with Fawn."

"I won't, but now that you've said she's going to be there, I wouldn't mind having the opportunity to talk to her and see how well she knew Fawn."

"That might be a good idea. Her body language should tell you a lot about how she felt about her." He scratched his nose. "One thing I keep coming back to. If she knew about the affair, she has motive to kill Fawn."

"True."

"Dr. Rhodes is adamant that she didn't know, but—"

"What if she did?"

He nodded.

Lacey shoved a strand of hair behind her ear. "Then I'll find that out while being as subtle as I possibly can."

"Perfect. You ready?"

"Yep." She grabbed the gift that had been delivered yesterday afternoon. She'd also ordered wrapping paper, tape and ribbon.

Creed had watched her take great care in wrapping the age-appropriate play gym before she'd bothered to eat breakfast. "She'll love it," he said.

Lacey shot him a half smile. "I'm nervous about going to a baby shower. How ridiculous is that?"

"Why?"

"Because I don't know who else will be there and what they may think or say about me being there. Dumb, huh?"

"I would never call your feelings dumb."

Scarlett padded over with her new lead in her mouth. Lacey had ordered that, too.

He looked at Lacey. "I think she plans on going with us."

"I'm fine with that, as long as you don't mind her staying in the car with you."

"Not at all." He led the way down the steps to his cruiser. "If you think of it as an assignment to get information, will that help settle your nerves?"

"Hmm. Maybe." She frowned. "Actually, yes."

"Then do that and let everything else

roll off your back. Although, I think you'll find you're having a good time."

She buckled Scarlett into the back and then herself into the passenger seat. Her tight expression pulled Creed up short. "What is it?"

Lacey shot him a sideways glance. "If I have a good time, I'll feel guilty."

"Because of Fawn."

She sighed. "I know life goes on, Creed. I really do. But it just seems wrong to enjoy it."

"What would Fawn want?"

A sad smile curved her lips. "I know what she'd want, but like I said, it's going to be hard—especially if we wind up not finding her killer."

"Oh, we'll find him. One way or another, we'll find him."

"And yet I'm taking the time to go to a shower, taking the lead investigator—that would be you—away from the case."

Creed snagged her fingers with his right hand while he drove toward Miranda's. "You're not taking me away from the case," he said. "I have my laptop and my phone. I'll be working. And when you're finished with the shower, let me know, and we'll compare notes."

She nodded as they pulled up to Miranda's house.

SEVENTEEN

Lacey walked up the steps to Miranda's home and rapped her knuckles against the door. It swung open and Jessica greeted her with wide eyes and her baby strapped to her chest. "You came!"

"You invited me. And I wanted to come."

"I'm so glad." Jessica grabbed her hand and pulled her through the foyer and into the kitchen. "Grab a snack and come visit."

Annie turned from the counter, a carrot stick dripping with ranch dressing in her hand. "Hey, Lacey. Glad to see you made it."

With an escort and an agenda, but she'd made it. Lacey wove her way through the kitchen and into the den, where she took in the expensive decor. Leather furniture softened by knitted afghans and colorful pillows graced the center of the room. The built-ins on the far wall held a large smart TV, books and family pictures. When she and Creed had been here last time, they'd not made it to this more relaxed area.

Jessica followed her and took a seat in the wingback chair. She had a stack of gifts beside her and Lacey added hers to it. She made small talk for a few minutes before another newcomer claimed the woman's attention. Lacey halfway listened while she let her gaze roam the other occupants, looking for one in particular. She'd never met Joanna Rhodes before, but would know her from the pictures in her husband's office.

Lacey spotted her at the food table. The woman had her dark blond hair pulled up in a stylish bun, with a few wispy strands loose around her temples. Her makeup had been expertly applied and Lacey figured her lipstick wouldn't dare fade even when she ate the small plate of food in her left hand. Lacey walked over and smiled. "Hello, Mrs. Rhodes."

The woman turned. "Hello." She frowned and smiled at the same time, and Lacey knew she was trying to pull a name from her memory.

"I'm Lacey Jefferson, Fawn's sister."

"Oh!" Surprise flashed briefly, along with another emotion Lacey couldn't put her finger on. "I was terribly sorry to hear about her death. Are they making any progress on finding who killed her?"

"Some." Lacey picked up a plate and two cucumber sandwiches. She needed some food before her blood sugar tanked again. After two bites, she wiped her mouth. "Were you and Fawn close?"

"No, not very. And it's Joanna. I knew Fawn, of course. She worked with my husband at the hospital."

"I know. Your husband had pictures in his office of Fawn and your family. That's how I recognized you. I would have thought you'd have been very close."

"No. Like I said, my husband and Fawn had a business relationship. That's all."

The woman's denial and lack of eye contact made it clear that she knew more than she wanted to say.

"Were Fawn and your husband—"

"I'm sorry." Joanna pointed over Lacey's shoulder. "I see someone I need to speak with about setting up a photography session for my new grandbaby. Excuse me."

She bolted away faster than if Lacey had announced she had the plague.

Lacey almost went after her, but speaking of pictures...

She walked to the built-in bookcases that encased the television and noted pictures of newborn TJ. One in particular caught her eye. Tucker Glenn held the baby close, the adoration on his face exposed for all the world to see. Only a couple of weeks old and already little TJ dominated the home. She smiled. She might not care for Tucker, but it was obvious he loved his son.

From there, she walked to the other side and froze. A framed group of ultrasound pictures rested on the bottom shelf. The same pictures she'd found in her house just before someone burned it down. Granted, most ultrasound pictures looked similar, but these were from the 3D set. And that little hand sticking up and waving at her was exactly the same as the one in Fawn's home.

Sickness swirled in the pit of her stomach while unanswered questions battled it out in her mind.

"Lacey?"

She turned to see Miranda looking at her, a frown creasing her forehead. "Hi."

"Glad you could make it. I noticed you looking at the pictures. Everything okay?"

"Oh yes." She had no idea what to think of what she was seeing, but she had enough sense to not blurt out her questions. "I... ah...was just thinking what a cutie TJ is. Very photogenic."

"Thanks. He is." An adoring smile smoothed her features. "You know, Tucker and I tried for a long time to have a child and it just never happened. We thought about adoption, but then I wound up pregnant with TJ and we got our happy ending."

"I see." Lacey forced a smile. "I'm so glad it all worked out for you. Where's TJ now?"

"Tucker took him to see his parents. I didn't think I could handle him and being an attentive hostess all at the same time."

"Well, I'm sure Tucker is enjoying the time with TJ."

"Very much so."

"Miranda, how well do you know Joanna?"

"Very well. We're great friends."

"Was she great friends with Fawn, too?"

"Of course. The three of us were together as much as possible. At least, we were before TJ was born and Joanna's new grandbaby arrived. But yes, the three of us were very close." Clouds flickered through her eyes. "I don't know what we'll do without Fawn. It won't ever be the same again. If I didn't have TJ, I'd—"

"Miranda?"

The call from across the room pulled the woman's attention from Lacey. "I guess that's my cue."

"Of course."

She left and Lacey drew in a steadying breath, then turned to snap a picture of the ultrasound photos. She aimed herself in the direction of the hall bath with a glance over her shoulder. Jessica had just begun to open her gifts. The gift she'd brought was at the end of the line, so she figured she had a few minutes to look around. What she was looking for, she had no idea, but if those pictures were of Fawn's baby, then that meant Miranda was claiming TJ was her child when…he wasn't. And that meant Miranda was hiding something. And so was her bestie, Joanna. Frustration gnawed at her. She kept gathering bits and pieces of information and couldn't figure out how to put them together to make sense in Fawn's death. So, she'd keep searching for more pieces.

The house was a large ranch but laid out simply. The main living area was in the center of two wings. It only took her a few minutes to walk back through the kitchen and down the hall to her right to peer in the rooms. She found TJ's nursery elaborately decorated with trains and planes. With a tight throat, she backed out and shut the door, then went to the next room.

The master. More pictures of TJ.

Lacey made her way past the festivities once more and walked into the other hall. A guest bath to her right, and to her left was a large guest room complete with sitting room and an en suite bath. The door was open, but she noted the dead bolt that locked with a key. Weird. Why would someone have a dead bolt on a bedroom door? The only reason she could come up with sent that "something's not right" feeling curling in the pit of her stomach. She stepped into the room and noted a television was mounted on the wall opposite the couch and a small desk was under the window.

Lacey caught a whiff of strawberry that reminded her of Fawn and decided it smelled a lot like Fawn's closet. Had her sister used this room? Maybe for the three months she'd dropped off the radar?

But...why?

And...had she been *locked* in here? But she'd had access to her phone and internet, so if she'd been held against her will, why hadn't she simply told someone once she'd been released? Or escaped?

The bits and pieces were driving her crazy. She needed the full picture.

She shut the door behind her, noting that it felt heavier than a typical interior door, but slid that fact to the back of her mind since she had no idea what—if anything—it could mean. She had to focus and be quick before she was missed.

Hopefully, if anyone noticed her absence, they'd think she'd simply slipped out and gone home. Lacey moved to the bathroom and she discovered it had been meticulously cleaned, but a bar of soap, like the kind her sister used, sat in the dish near the faucet.

Heart in her throat, she pulled out her phone while she walked to the closet. She opened the door and sucked in a gasp. Hanging on a hanger toward the back was a pregnancy suit. In fact, there were several different sizes going from smaller to bigger.

The pieces started to fall into place. Miranda had faked her pregnancy and now had Fawn's baby. Lacey knew it; she just didn't know how to prove it. She exited the closet, walked to the desk and noted the Bible in the corner. She wondered if it was there for show, then pulled the middle drawer open. Empty.

As were all of the other drawers.

She checked the dresser and found linens and several items of stylish maternity clothes. Had Miranda worn those with her fake pregnancy body? Lacey pulled out her phone to take pictures of everything. She tapped Creed's number. When it didn't ring after several seconds, she checked the signal.

Nothing. "What?" How was that possible?

She walked to the door and turned the knob.

Locked.

Her heart dropped.

Someone had locked her in the room.

Creed had walked the perimeter of the Glenn home with Scarlett, letting the dog stretch her legs and run for a few minutes. It was a huge party, big enough to make Creed wonder if the entire town had shown up, and cars were parked in the drive as well as the grassy area to the side of the house. He and Scarlett dodged the vehicles, and a few newly arriving ladies, and made their way back to the cruiser.

As soon as he opened the door, planning to get Scarlett settled and to make some calls about Fawn's case, Regina called him.

"What's up?" he asked.

"I talked to the ultrasound office. It's a very swanky place that caters to the rich and famous. A well-to-do couple funded the place in the hopes that it would attract pregnant ladies who wouldn't otherwise go to that type of place. All that aside, one of the workers said she remembered Fawn, and that she was accompanied by another woman."

"Did she say who?"

"No. And she was cut off from saying more by another worker. And *that* person said they don't have security cameras."

Creed paused. "I'm not sure I believe that."

"I didn't either, especially since their biggest attraction to their clientele is their confidential and privacy assurances. Seems to me that they'd want cameras for the added security. Regardless, we're still looking into that. After some digging, I found out they also work with some high-priced adoption lawyers. Everything is handled privately and quickly. But the security footage was my main focus. I called a friend of mine who's a cop about an hour away from there and asked if he could verify that. And if they do have cameras, then we needed the footage."

"They think they're protecting their clients by hiding anything that might reveal who's used their services."

"Yeah."

"Let me know what he finds out."

"Will do. And before I go, I've got some information on Gillian Fields. She works for a medical equipment supply company on Main Street. I talked to her about her gym card and she said she noticed it was missing after a visit to the hospital."

"Weird."

"Yes."

She hung up, and Creed noticed more people leaving the shower. Ladies had been coming and going ever since Lacey had gone inside, but it seemed like an exceptionally large number were climbing into their cars and heading out.

But no sign of Lacey.

He sent her a text, then scanned the

two ladies exiting the front door. Both wore frowns and both glanced backward as though in concern. Lacey was still in there. She was probably talking to Miranda or something. When he spotted Carmen Houser, he climbed out of the car and walked toward her. "Hey, have you seen Lacey?" He and Carmen had graduated high school together. She worked as a teller at the local bank.

"I saw her come in but didn't get a chance to speak to her before she disappeared."

"I'm sorry—what?"

She laughed. "Not literally. I saw her talking to Joanna, then Miranda, and I got distracted when Jessica opened my present. By the time I went looking for her, she was already gone."

Gone? "Gone where?"

"No idea, Creed. I don't have her on my list of friends I track."

He wasn't even going to ask her if she was serious. "Thanks."

"Although, to be honest, she might still

be in there. Miranda wasn't feeling well all of a sudden, so we decided to leave."

"Not feeling well? She okay?"

"Yes, I think so. She just got really light-headed and dizzy and said she had to lie down. Then Joanna said she wasn't feeling great, and at that point, I was afraid it might be something in the food."

"Uh-oh."

"Exactly. I hadn't eaten anything and wasn't about to at that point." She paused. "So, are you two a thing again?"

He shot her a tight smile. "Thanks for the information, Carmen. Good to see you."

She laughed and walked toward her car while Creed pondered whether or not he should go in. He sighed. Carmen hadn't seemed concerned about anything other than getting food poisoning, so he'd give Lacey a few more minutes, then go check on her.

EIGHTEEN

Lacey beat on the door until her hands hurt. She'd pounded and cried out for the past five minutes and no one had come. She finally decided the room was soundproof. Which chilled her. Why would they need a soundproof room?

The lock clicked and Lacey spun. Miranda stepped inside and shut the door behind her. In her right hand, she held a gun that she lifted and pointed at Lacey.

"Miranda?" she whispered. "You killed Fawn."

"It was an accident." Miranda's eyes filled with tears for a brief moment before they disappeared, and her gaze hardened.

"Then why cover it up?"

"Are you kidding me? I would have been

arrested. Gone to jail. Possibly lost my son."

"You mean Fawn's son."

Miranda gasped and paled. "No. *My* son."

"You may call him your son, but Fawn gave birth to him."

"How do you know?"

"I found a copy of the ultrasound pictures in Fawn's guest room closet."

"That's not possible. She *never* left here. Not for the full three months. She gave birth in that bed right there."

"Well, I guess she managed to make copies somehow, because they were in her closet." Lacey's fingers clenched into fists. "*Why* did you kill her?"

Miranda shuddered and Lacey fingered her phone in her pocket, wishing she could somehow get out of the room and call for help. "I didn't mean to. She was saying stuff like she was making a horrible mistake, that she wanted him back and wanted to help figure out a plan to do that." A scoff slipped from her. "There was no way that was happening. I'd gone through the whole charade of being pregnant and having the child and—" She waved a hand. "There was no way. When I refused to discuss it, she said she was sorry, but that she had to do the right thing, the honest thing. That I needed to give TJ back to her and come clean. I was stunned. I couldn't believe she'd turn on me like that. We were at her house in the yard. She was planting flowers. The shovel was leaning against the side of the house and I grabbed it and..."

"Hit her," Lacey said, her voice dull. Almost monotone. She'd wanted to know what had happened and now she knew. "And then you strangled her to make sure she never woke up."

Miranda's eyes widened. "What? Strangle her? No!"

"The ME says you did."

She frowned. "I hit her, and she grabbed her head—there was so much blood that I was...shocked. I couldn't believe I'd done that. She screamed at me that I'd lost it. I still held the shovel and I guess she thought I was going to hit her again, so she ran toward the woods…" Her eyes darkened. "I called Tucker, hysterical. He came to the house and went to the woods looking for Fawn. He said he found her on the ground. That she'd fallen and bled out." Miranda shoved a hand against her mouth. "I never meant for her to get hurt, but I couldn't let her take my baby."

"Miranda, Fawn was strangled. The ME said the blow from the shovel wouldn't have killed her."

Miranda's brows pulled tighter across the bridge of her nose and confusion clouded her eyes. "But…" Realization and horror dawned. "Tucker," she whispered.

"Yeah, Tucker." Miranda's hand shook and her finger twitched on the trigger. "So, knowing that you're not a murderer, are you going to kill me and become one?"

"I… I don't know. I have to think." A tear slipped down her cheek. "Tucker said she was dead when he found her, that I'd killed her, and we had to hide her. He covered her up out in the woods where he said he found her, but said he was going to have to move her. He was pacing and talking and trying to come up with a story for her disappearance. I told him that we didn't need a story because we weren't going to know anything about where she went."

"So, he panic-buried her," Lacey murmured. They'd been right about that. "Why shoot at us? Was that you?"

"No..."

"Who?"

"That was James."

"Tucker's brother?" She remembered him from the hospital.

"Tucker hadn't had a chance to move her, and when he saw where the hunt for Hank was leading, he called James and told him to scare y'all away from the area. He said he shot at the shed, hoping to distract you."

"But Scarlett found her anyway."

"Stupid dog. If you hadn't brought her

into the picture, Fawn would have just stayed missing."

"You had to know I'd come looking for her."

Miranda shrugged. "I figured you would, but I also thought that if I could just act normal, you'd eventually give up and go away."

"But I didn't, so you tried to run me over, shoot me with a crossbow and burn me in my home."

"Tucker was in a panic and James would do anything for Tucker. So, the two of them did all that."

"Who did you tell we were going to the gym?"

"James. I told him Tucker needed him to make you go away."

"So, he stole a key card and attacked me in the locker room." She rubbed a hand down her face. Well, she'd wanted all the pieces to the puzzle, but this wasn't quite the way she'd wanted to get them. "Who burned Fawn's house down?"

"That was James's idea. They were looking for Fawn's journal. She wrote in it constantly. When they couldn't find it in her house, he told Tucker they just needed to burn it down. With you in it."

Lacey shuddered at the coldness of it all. "Where's the journal?"

"I guess it was in the house. We searched all over the place here and couldn't find it. There's no telling what she wrote and we couldn't have it found in case—"

"She wrote the truth?"

"Yes," Miranda whispered.

Lacey gripped her temples and shook her head. "I can't believe this. I can't believe Fawn agreed to be locked in a room for three months." She couldn't believe any of it.

"She knew my need for control," Miranda admitted. "I was petrified she'd change her mind. She agreed to the lock, the soundproofing, the cell signal blocker, everything. All to reassure me—and it worked. She even let me keep her laptop."

"But I talked to her on the phone. She answered my texts."

334 Following the Trail

"I was there for every conversation and I monitored every text."

"And the ultrasounds?"

"A friend's clinic. No questions asked."

It was scary how well she'd worked to cover her tracks. "Creed's waiting outside as we speak," Lacey said. "In fact, he'll probably come looking for me shortly."

"Then I guess we'd better make sure he doesn't find you just yet until I figure out what to do."

She backed out of the room and shut the door faster than Lacey could move.

She walked to the twin bed and stared at it, picturing Fawn laboring to give birth. All alone, maybe a little afraid in spite of all her medical knowledge. The rage shuddered through her and she grabbed the comforter and pulled it off, letting out a harsh scream. She grabbed the pillows and, with another yell, tossed them across the room. One landed on the desk, knocking the lamp to the floor and shattering the Tiffany design. Next came the sheets. Then she hefted the top mattress and sent it crashing into the pictures on the wall. They tumbled to the floor. The sound of the breaking glass was incredibly satisfying.

She started for the box springs and froze, breathing hard, face wet with sweat and tears. A small journal with a cover like the one she'd given Fawn lay there as though waiting for Lacey to find it. She'd given Fawn the little book the same time she'd gifted her the bracelet.

This was what everyone had been so desperate to find and it was under their noses the whole time. Lacey snatched up the journal, took it to the desk and flopped into the chair. She had to think. To escape. But she'd been all over the room and attached bath and could find no way out. Maybe Fawn's words could help her. Once she caught her breath, she opened the cover and began to read.

Well, I might as well use this to pass the time. I have no idea why Lacey gave me a journal, but maybe it was for this moment, this...time in my life.

My life. Wow. I've really done a number on it—in addition to all the issues my father's actions have left me with. But maybe this is the way to fix it and make things right for at least one person whose life he ruined. Tucker Glenn. I never thought I'd call him friend, but over the last few weeks, he's been different. Kind. Less scary. Which is nice. I wish I'd had the strength to leave Timber Creek like Lacey, but, after Dad did his thing, I felt like I had to stay. To make amends. Which is stupid, but nevertheless, the feeling is real. I'm not the one who's the criminal—and yet, I guess I am. Seven months pregnant and I'm participating in an unbelievable scheme. I seriously can't believe I'm doing this. But...it's a situation of my own making. I freely admit that. I made a choice that I wish desperately I could take back. A choice with consequences

I thought about but risked anyway. A choice that has led to the deception— and pain—of many people. So, I guess I'm not so different from my father after all. Lacey would be mortified. Ashamed and disappointed. Which is why I can't tell her. And why I'm really starting to hate myself.

Lacey stifled a sob and slammed the book shut. She rose and paced to the window. She tried to raise it yet again. And again, she was met with unmoving resistance. She grabbed the desk chair, hefted it and slammed it against the window. The chair bounced off the glass and fell to the floor.

"Argh!"

She went to the book once again, reading and pacing, absorbing Fawn's words in one part of her mind, while the other part worked furiously on an escape plan.

The truth is, I don't think I can actually go through with this. Then again, how can I not? I feel I have to at this point. After all, what am I going to do with a child? Charles doesn't want him, and I understand that. I don't hold that against him. And Miranda has gone through such a massive deception of pretending to be pregnant. The woman deserves an Oscar. Although, I had no idea until a few days ago what she was doing. I thought she was hiding out so she could claim the child as her own. I was partially right. She definitely wants to claim the baby as hers, but she's been parading around in a pregnancy suit! She's worn it 24/7 apparently. Unbelievable.

I've been reading the Bible again and feeling convinced that I'm doing a terrible thing. I don't want to do this. I want to find a way to keep my son—I've named him Hudson Christopher simply because I like the name—and give him the family that he deserves. I'm definitely not sure about Miranda as a mother. She's incredibly control-

ling, and I'm worried she'll control this baby right into a psychiatric ward.

Fawn went on to talk about how she'd agreed to stay in the room and basically be Miranda and Tucker's prisoner in order to appease Miranda's obsessive fear that someone would find out Fawn was pregnant.

I've about had enough, Fawn wrote.

Lacey flipped the page. Fawn had been studying the Bible and growing closer to God.

One thing about being confined in this room is it's certainly given me some downtime. Time to read and to pray and to reflect. I'm so thankful God still loves me even when I'm not lovable. I should have told Lacey about the baby. She would have offered to help, but that's the problem. I don't want to disrupt her life when she's finally found some peace. And if I tell her about the baby, I'll have to tell her that I'm in love with a married man. A man who is thirty years older than I am. A man who has grandchildren and a very possessive wife.

The dead bolt clicked and this time she heard it. Lacey stuffed the journal in the desk drawer and shut it. She turned as the door swung open.

Creed glanced at his watch, then his phone. No answering text from Lacey and the last guest from the shower had left five minutes ago. He climbed out of the cruiser once more and walked up the steps to knock on the door.

When it swung open, Miranda stood there looking a bit frazzled. "Hello, Creed. What can I do for you?"

"Everything okay?"

She blinked and tucked a stray strand of hair behind her ear. "Of course. Why?"

"Heard there was some kind of food poisoning issue?"

She laughed, but the sound was forced

and Creed's cop senses tingled. "Yes. A small one. We think the salmon cakes were tainted. We thought it best to end the shower early just in case it was more than food poisoning. We certainly don't need to spread any illness that might be going around."

"I understand. I just wanted to check in with Lacey. She's not answering her phone."

"Oh no." Miranda smacked her forehead in a very un-Miranda-like move. "I was supposed to call you and let you know that her phone was doing something strange and not sending texts for some reason. She left a while ago to drive one of the ladies home."

"Which one?"

"I'm not sure, but she said to let you know she'd do that, then call you to pick her up."

That didn't sound right, but knowing Lacey, she would definitely offer to help if someone needed it. However, in light of the current situation, there was no way she'd just take off with him right there. "Are you sure about this? That she left with a woman?"

"I'm sure."

"But you don't know which one?"

"Um, maybe Joanna Rhodes? I'm not sure, but they just left a few minutes ago. If you head toward town, you might catch them. Maybe? I'm sorry, Creed. I really am. It's been chaos in here for the past twenty minutes or so. I haven't kept up with everyone's comings and goings." She pressed a hand against her head and said, "Now, I've a ferocious migraine coming on. I've got to run."

With that, she shut the door in his face. Two seconds later, Tucker's sedan pulled into the drive. He got out and stopped short when he eyed Creed. "Everything okay?"

"Yeah, I think so. Just trying to track down Lacey."

"Oh."

"Where's the baby?"

"I left him with my mother. She offered

to babysit so Miranda and I could have a night out. Only Miranda says she's not feeling well, so I'm just going to check on her."

He backed toward the door and Creed waved, then hurried to his cruiser. He would try to find Joanna and Lacey first on the off chance Miranda's story was true. But something was going on. He didn't know what it was, but he had a feeling he was going to need backup.

NINETEEN

For several moments after the door opened, she and Tucker eyed each other. Then her gaze went to the weapon in his hand, absently noting it was the same one Miranda had threatened her with earlier. The fury returned. This man had cold-bloodedly killed her sister, and not an ounce of remorse was reflected in his eyes.

In fact, Lacey was quite sure he planned to do the same thing to her.

He shot a glance at the room, noting the destruction, and his jaw tightened.

"Where's Miranda?" Lacey asked.

"Doesn't matter. Let's go."

"Where?"

"Just walk until I tell you to stop. We're going out the back of the house, not the front."

Since getting out of the room worked in her favor, she did as he instructed and slipped out into the hallway. He stepped up behind her and pressed the gun against her left kidney. Defense moves played in her head, but now wasn't the time. They were going out of the house. She mentally mapped the area. If she could get to the woods—

"Go. Faster."

Creed was out there. All she had to do was get his attention. She picked up the pace and entered the kitchen. "Through the door to the right and down the steps."

Lacey followed his instructions and made her way down the stairs, her eyes on the door just ahead. As soon as she was out the door, she'd scream her head off and hope Creed came running.

The gun pressed harder against her back as though Tucker could read her thoughts. "You killed Fawn and now you're going to kill me. Are you going to go after Creed and the rest of the sheriff's department? Because they all know you're involved."

He laughed. "Nice try, but no, they don't."

"Fawn said you'd started being nicer to her, that you weren't as bad as you used to be in high school."

"Stop."

She did so.

"When did Fawn say that? Because she never once, in the last three months, mentioned me or Miranda. So, when would she have said that?"

She turned slightly to look back at him. "We talked all the time before those three months she was your prisoner."

"But I didn't really start being nice to her until she was living here. So, how did you know that?" His eyes narrowed and he lifted the gun to press it against her head. "You found the journal, didn't you?"

Lacey froze. She'd messed up.

"Where is it?"

"I don't know."

His hand shot out and he slammed her head against the wall. Stars flashed in front of her eyes and she cried out, fighting a sudden wave of nausea. "Where is it?"

"That's why you burned my house to the ground." She spit at him. "Well, I won't tell you where it is. If you kill me, I'll take great satisfaction in knowing that evidence is out there, detailing what you put my sister through."

For a moment, she thought he might pull the trigger. Instead, he shot a look at the clock on the wall over the washing machine. "Open the door," he said. "And don't think you can run to Creed. He left a few minutes ago."

Dread centered itself in her gut and stayed there. So that was why Tucker was moving her. Creed would want to search the house. She twisted the knob and he shoved her out into the sunshine. "Go."

"Where?"

"To the barn. Hurry up."

The gun slipped from her head and Lacey spun in a smooth move and used her forearm to knock the weapon from him. He yelled and dived for the gun the same time Lacey did. He wrapped his fingers around the grip, and she knew she didn't have the strength to wrestle it away from him. She bolted to her feet and kicked him in the face. His nose crunched, and a raw scream ripped from his throat. One hand went to his face while the other lifted the weapon. She kicked again and caught his wrist. The gun spun out of his grip and she whirled, racing for the barn. If she could get to the road, she could flag someone down.

Something slammed into her back and she went down with a hard grunt. Pain rippled through her right shoulder, but she tried to scramble away from him. His fingers twisted in her hair and another lightning bolt of agony shot through her head. She froze, panting, tears sliding down her temples as she blinked up at the sky.

"Don't move." His order vibrated with a tightly leashed fury. Lacey stayed still. She couldn't move anyway without him taking a chunk of her hair and skin with him. "Walk to the barn. Now."

Lacey did as ordered, fighting the urge to be sick. She let him get her to the barn.

Barns had all kinds of things that could be used as weapons. She'd find one and end this once and for all.

But when they got there, he walked her past a motorcycle, a golf cart and a pitchfork she wanted to grab and couldn't. He shoved her into a room and held the weapon on her while he blocked the door. "You have until I come back to tell me where that journal is. If you don't, I'm going to go after your old boyfriend. Creed won't know what hit him."

"He suspects you're involved in Fawn's death. He'll be on guard."

His eyes blazed, but he didn't shoot her. Instead, he smirked. "Guess we'll find out."

He shut the door and locked it.

Which meant Lacey was trapped once more.

Creed pulled to a stop out of sight of the Glenn home. He let Scarlett out from her spot in the back and fastened the lead to her harness. As he'd feared, he hadn't found Joanna or Lacey. When he felt like he'd been sent on a fool's errand and decided Lacey was still in the house somewhere, he'd done a one-eighty and called Regina to bring him something of Lacey's that would have her scent on it. He didn't know if it would be necessary, but better to be prepared than not. Katherine had let Regina into Lacey's temporary apartment and Regina had grabbed the pillow from Lacey's bed. Then she met him a mile away from the Glenns' house.

"Let me go up to the front door first," he said into his radio, "and ask to search the house. Stay out of sight until I need you."

"Ten-four. Mac just pulled up, too. Ben is almost here."

He clicked to Scarlett. "All right, girl, I hope you can do this without Lacey." At Lacey's name, Scarlett's ears lifted and she looked around. "Yeah, I want to see her, too. Let's go find her."

He knocked on the door and waited. Footsteps sounded, the curtain to his right moved, and the door swung open, revealing Miranda's agitated form. "What do you want now? I told you Lacey's not here."

"Then you won't mind if I search your house?"

Her eyes went wide. "Search my house?" She nearly sputtered the words. "Absolutely not."

"Fine. Then I'm getting a warrant. Lacey wouldn't just leave without telling where she was going."

"And you think she's here?"

"I do. Now, do I get a warrant or do you let me in?"

"Let him in," a voice said from behind Miranda. "She's not here."

Creed pushed past Miranda with Scarlett at his heels. He had the pillowcase in a bag in his left hand. Tucker stepped out of the shadows, holding an ice pack on his face. He had two black eyes. Creed did a double take. "What happened to you, man?"

"I was in the barn and a two-by-four fell out of the loft and smacked me in the face."

"Leave the dog outside," Miranda said. "I don't want that filthy creature in my house."

"Sorry," Creed said, "but the dog goes with me." He held the bag out to her and tried to remember the exact commands Lacey had used with her. "Scent, Scarlett."

"What are you doing?" Miranda fairly screeched.

"Letting Scarlett get Lacey's scent."

"What? No! Get her out!"

Creed knew the others were listening to the entire conversation. His only concern was whether one of them—or both of them—had a weapon. He didn't dare underestimate Tucker. The man was a hunter and had weapons. "Tucker?"

The man waved a hand. "Fine. Search the house. Knock yourself out."

"Thank you." Into the radio, he said, "Regina, can you come in and sit with the Glenns while I check the house?"

Tucker glowered. Miranda twisted her hands and shot looks at her husband that Creed couldn't decipher. Regina stepped inside the house and Creed said, "They've given me verbal permission to search. Just hang out here and I'll be right back."

"Great."

To Scarlett, he said, "Scarlett, find Lacey."

The dog circled the den and then stuck her nose to the floor, then the air, and started for the back of the house. In a lower voice, he said, "Stand by." Scarlett took him through the kitchen and straight to a door. She sat and waited for him to open it. As soon as she could scoot through, she did and scrambled down the stairs. He kept going, giving her the space to work. She wanted out the door at the bottom, and again, he opened it and Scarlett darted out.

"Hey! Stop!"

Regina's shout from the other side of the house pulled him to a halt. Tucker was racing across the yard toward the barn, and just beyond him, he could see Lacey sprinting for the trees.

"Lacey!"

She spun and saw him. Tucker aimed for

the barn. "Tucker, stop!" Creed yelled, not expecting the man to listen. And he didn't.

Lacey stopped, spotted Tucker and bolted after him. What was she *doing*?

Tucker disappeared into the barn. Creed reached the door and barely escaped being mowed down when Tucker burst from the barn driving a golf cart. He headed toward the trees that would take him to one of the back roads. Lacey changed direction and raced toward Tucker once more. He realized immediately what she planned. "Lacey, no!"

But she did exactly what he thought she was going to do. She launched herself into the passenger side and kept going, propelling herself into Tucker and sending them both falling from the driver's side to the ground. The golf cart continued at top speed away from the scene while Tucker and Lacey rolled. When they stopped, Tucker pulled back an arm. Scarlett hurled herself at the duo and chomped down on Tucker's forearm before he could land the blow to Lacey's face.

He screamed and Lacey bucked the man off. Scarlett held on, a low growl escaping her. "Get her off me!"

"Scarlett, release!"

Scarlett let go and backed up, her eyes on the man who'd attacked her beloved mistress. Creed hurried forward to grab the man's arms and pull them behind him. He pressed the cuffs around Tucker's wrists before the guy could get himself together to put up a fight. "Tucker Glenn, you're under arrest." He recited the man's rights and pulled him to his feet.

Regina stepped up beside them, breathing hard from her run across the field. "He got the drop on me."

"It's okay. It's the last drop he'll get. What about Miranda?"

"Ben's got her. She realized Tucker was trying to escape and run out on her and started singing like the proverbial canary."

He nodded and looked at Lacey. "We got them."

"Yeah," she whispered. "We got them.

And his brother, James, is involved in everything, too."

"I'll have someone pick him up before he gets wind of everything."

"I've got Tucker," Regina said. "You take care of Lacey."

Creed walked to Scarlett and gave her a belly rub, then pulled the tennis ball from his pocket and threw it. She raced after it and Creed gathered Lacey into his arms. "I love you, Lacey Lee Jefferson."

She stilled and sighed. Then looked up with watery eyes. "I love you, too, Sheriff Creed Payne."

"Good. I've decided to turn in my resignation and move to Charlotte, if that's what it takes to be with you."

She pulled back and gaped at him. "Um, no, I've decided to move back to Timber Creek. I'm going to rebuild the house and plant a big ole tree in honor of Fawn. And—" she blew out a low breath "—and raise her son. Her baby is TJ, Creed."

"How do you know?"

"I found her journal. I'll let you read

some of the entries, but she named him Hudson Christopher. Social services has gone to get him. I feel terrible about taking him away from the people who thought they were his grandparents—because they really do love him—but I won't take him out of their lives if they want to see him." She bit her lip and studied him, uncertainty swimming in her gaze. "Is that a deal breaker?"

"Are you kidding me?" Creed could barely speak around the emotion swelling in his throat. "I would love Hudson with all my heart. As if he was my own."

"You've never even met him."

"I don't have to. He's a part of you and Fawn. And he's an innocent child. A gift. I don't take that lightly."

She stood on tiptoe to seal her lips to his. Creed's heart pounded and prayers of thanksgiving whispered heavenward. He pulled her closer, hoping she could feel his love for her in the kiss. He deepened it, sweeping his hands over her hair—and feeling the knot on her head. He pulled back. "You're hurt."

"Kissing you makes me forget about it. Don't stop."

He gave a short laugh but cupped her face. "We need to get you to a doctor. You could have a concussion."

"Then we can call Katherine, but I have a feeling her orders are going to be the same ones the ER doc gave Mac."

"You're stubborn."

"At least you know what you're getting into."

"I do. So, let's make it official." He dropped to one knee and took her hand. Her eyes widened and her cheeks turned pink. "Lacey Lee, will you marry—"

"Yes!" She laid another kiss on him and Creed couldn't contain the bubble of laughter welling up.

He leaned back and she shot him a sheepish look. "Sorry. You can finish asking the question and I promise not to interrupt."

"Aw, Lacey, you can interrupt me anytime."

In fact, she could spend a lifetime interrupting him and it wouldn't be long enough. "I love you, Lacey."

"I love you, Creed."

TWENTY

Four weeks later

Fawn's last journal entry:

> *I suppose I should write down some things in case something weird happens and I die during childbirth. Unlikely, I know, but I'm a doctor and my mind morbidly goes there.*
>
> *Anyway, should I die, the whole process of dispersing my property will be extremely easy. And even though I've forgiven my mother and plan to call her when I can think straight again, everything goes to my sister, Lacey Lee Jefferson. Everything. My will is in my safety-deposit box at High Point Bank in Timber Creek.*

And, if there's a way, should I no longer be on this earth, I'd want Lacey to raise my son, not Miranda Glenn. Somehow, I have to get out of this deal I've made with them. I just can't figure out how. Telling them "I've changed my mind" just doesn't seem right. They've gone to great lengths to pull off this deception. I'm actually quite stunned at it.

And I'm a little scared of Tucker, to be honest. I'm not sure what his reaction might be should I tell him I want to back out. I know Miranda would go completely bonkers. So, for now, I'll continue thinking and praying about this. Please, God, I need Your help— an answer in the midst of this situation I've created. Although I don't wish to move, I've gone ahead and done the interviews for the jobs in Charlotte per Miranda and Tucker's wishes, but I doubt I'll take one of them. If, for some reason, I can't reverse all of this, at least I can still watch Hudson grow up if I'm living in the same town.

I wish I could talk to Lacey, but I gave my word to say nothing. And I won't. But I want to. I love you, Lacey. Maybe one day, I'll be able to tell you everything.

Lacey grunted and set the journal aside, tears blurring her vision. "He'll be happy here, Fawn. I promise."

Construction had already started on her childhood home and it was going to be finished in record time. Like probably within the next two weeks. Crews made up of locals and some hired hands had been working practically around the clock to get it ready, and Lacey was simply bowled over by the generous people in this town. And so thankful to them.

Hudson, who'd been sleeping in the bassinet next to her, let out his "I'm hungry" cry, and Lacey stuffed a bottle between his lips. She'd learned to be prepared when he was due to wake up, because he acted like he was starving from the moment his eyes popped open. He was a funny little guy and she saw Fawn in him every time he smiled. He had her eyes and her smile, but he had his father's nose.

She and Hudson had been living in the apartment above the clinic for the past four weeks. Her mother had flown in from California with her husband and come for the funeral. She'd stayed in town for another week, reconnecting with Lacey and spoiling her grandson. Lacey smiled. It had been a good visit. A healing one.

A knock on the door curved her lips even further. Scarlett lifted her head and perked her ears toward the door. "Come on in!" Lacey said.

Creed entered and made a beeline for the bassinet, stopping to plant a kiss on her lips and scratch Scarlett's ears. Then he picked up the baby and held the bottle while Hudson drained it. Creed looked at her. "How are you doing?"

"Aw, you know I have good days and bad." Just speaking the words caused tears to threaten, but she held them back. "Today's not so great. I'm mad at her, Creed," she said, her voice low.

"I know."

"All of this could have been avoided if she'd just been honest."

"Agreed, but sometimes we have to learn things the hard way. Unfortunately, Fawn didn't get a chance to learn from her mistakes."

Lacey fell silent. Being mad at Fawn wouldn't accomplish anything. Her sister was gone. But she'd left a precious piece of herself behind and Lacey knew her anger with her sister would fade in time. "I can't believe Dr. Rhodes really agreed to sign away his rights to Hudson."

Child Protection Services had picked the baby up from Tucker's mother's home and were waiting to hand him over to Lacey as next of kin when she'd come home from the hospital after her encounter with Tucker and the golf cart.

"He doesn't want it known—especially by his wife—that he was unfaithful. Although, I think he'll tell her at some point. He seemed remorseful and repentant." He pulled the empty bottle from the baby's mouth and settled the little guy on his shoulder for a burp. "But for the next eighteen years, Rhodes has agreed not to contact you or Hudson, but said if Hudson wanted to know about him later, he'd consider it."

She nodded. "I want him to know the truth one day. I want him to know everything. But mostly, I want him to know he's loved." As always, the tears hovered near the surface, but she was getting quite proficient at keeping them from falling. "So very loved."

"He's loved," Creed said. "In fact, I almost can't remember life before him." He swallowed and Lacey loved that he wasn't hesitant to show his emotion. "And I'm ready to set the date when you are."

"I'm ready."

"Next week?"

She laughed. "Maybe not quite that ready, but next month should work."

His gaze lingered. "I can't quite believe this is happening," Creed said. "I'm so sorry for the reason you came home, but I think Fawn would be thrilled at the way everything turned out."

Lacey nodded. "She would. She'd wanted me to come home for years." She sighed. "And I wish I had, but..."

He settled on the sofa beside her. "The dogs are all set up at your place in their nice new area and are ready to continue their training. We've got the funds approved to hire one more K-9 handler, Isabelle is all set to watch this little guy while we're at work, and your first day is tomorrow. How are you feeling?"

"Excited." Butterflies swarmed in her belly, but she was ready. "Like it's the beginning of something really, really good."

Creed kissed her with a hint of restrained passion that made her head swim. When he pulled back, he leaned his forehead against hers. "I'm all for new beginnings because I'm *beginning* to be addicted to kissing you."

"I know exactly what you mean."

Joy exploded within her as they shared another lingering kiss. Lacey knew she might have initially followed the trail to find her sister's killer, but that trail had also led her home and back into Creed's arms. And for that, she'd be forever grateful.

Scarlett barked her agreement.

* * * * *

If you enjoyed this story, look for these other books by Lynette Eason:

Peril on the Ranch
Mountain Fugitive

Dear Reader,

I'm so blessed you picked up this book to read Creed and Lacey's story. I've been trying to get those two together for a while now. And though it took a tragedy to bring them to their senses, at least they learned from their mistakes. They learned forgiveness is essential for happiness. This is the last story in the Timber Creek series and I do hope you've managed to get your hands on the previous two. The first one is *Peril on the Ranch* and then *Mountain Fugitive*. I had a lot of fun writing about the people in this small town and I'll miss them, but my heart smiles knowing they all live happily ever after. I pray the stories make you smile, too.

Happy reading and God bless,
Lynette